That Time I Kinda Killed a Guy

Val Fremden Strikes Again, Volume 1

Margaret Lashley

Published by Zazzy Ideas, Inc., 2023.

Copyright

Contents

More Mysteries by Margaret Lashley

Available on Amazon in Your Choice of Ebook, Paperback, Hardback, or Audiobook.

Val Fremden Strikes Again Humorous Mysteries (in order)

- That Time I Kinda Killed a Guy
- There's Something About Gary
- Show Me the Funny Money
- More to come!

https://www.amazon.com/dp/B0CG648N16

New to Val Fremden? Don't miss the series that started it all! Val Fremden Midlife Mysteries (Nine-Book Series)
https://www.amazon.com/gp/product/B07FK88WQ3
Absolute Zero (The Val Fremden Prequel)
https://www.amazon.com/dp/B06ZXYK776
Doreen Diller Mystery Trilogy (Three-Book Series)
https://www.amazon.com/gp/product/B0B2X3G3G7
Freaky Florida Investigations (Eight-Book Series)
https://www.amazon.com/gp/product/B07RL4G8GZ
Mind's Eye Investigators (Two-Book Series)
https://www.amazon.com/gp/product/B07ZR6NW2N

Prologue (Or Maybe I Should Call it a Disclaimer)

Hi. I'm Val Fremden.

Despite being on a last-name basis with most of the cops in town, I'm *not* a criminal. I'll have you know, to date, I've been cleared on all charges.

Every. Single. One.

Why I keep ending up in the middle of so many screwball situations remains a mystery to me. But I do have a theory.

I believe that "the powers that be" decided to bestow upon me the perfect combination of curiosity, skepticism, impatience, and pig-headed determination that makes it darn near *impossible* for me to resist going to bat for the underdogs of this world.

Sure, I'd be the first to admit that quite often I find myself in way over my head. But maybe that's what being an "under" dog is all about.

Lately, however, I've begun to wonder if *I* might be the biggest underdog of all time. I mean, why else would the Universe keep throwing me these crazy curveballs?

Given my long list of flaws and foibles, I've still managed to keep a pretty good batting average.

To date, by hook or crook, I've helped solve over a dozen oddball mysteries. Some say that makes me a bit more seasoned at the game. I tend to agree—especially if you count the salt and pepper in my hair.

Anyway, by my clock it's just about time for my life to go hilariously off the rails. I cordially invite you to come along for the ride.

But be sure and buckle up, my friend.

You have been warned.

Chapter One

I used to take comfort in being a complete nobody. Three days ago, I was just your average, fifty-something, mostly law-abiding citizen. Seriously. What were the odds the universe would single *me* out for infamy?

But it did. Last Thursday.

I swear, I was just minding my own business when it happened. Suddenly, my ordinary little life was smashed to smithereens by a gigantic naked guy wielding an old-timey alarm clock.

Well, that's how this whole crazy mess got *started*, anyway ...

••••

"VAL FREMDEN?"

The sharp, nasal voice pierced my scattered thoughts. I glanced up to see a tired, frizzy-haired woman clutching a clipboard.

I smiled and raised my hand. "Uh ... that's me."

"Come on. Follow me."

I stood and dusted the cheese-cracker crumbs from my polyester pants. Then I shot a triumphant smile at the taut-skinned, smartly dressed young hopefuls milling about the waiting room at Tiffany's Temp Agency.

Ha! My underwear is older than most of you kids.

Slinging my vinyl purse over my shoulder, I glanced around the fresh-faced crowd. "Good luck, y'all. And don't worry. I'm sure they just wanted someone more seasoned for the job."

"Yeah, right," a size-two blonde uttered through a pair of full, pouty lips. I used to have a pair just like them sometime before she was born. Then the little squirt went and dropped the M word on me. "Ma'am, if you were any more *seasoned*, they'd have to serve you with a side of Pepto-Bismol."

I huffed with indignation. "I'll have you know, Miss Smarty Pants, that around here they call me *The Closer*."

A gasp sounded from somewhere in the room. Lipstick-laden mouths fell open. Fake eyelashes fluttered.

"So, *you're* the one," Miss Smarty Pants whispered breathlessly.

I arched an eyebrow for dramatic effect. "That's right. And don't you forget it."

"Fremden?" the lady with the clipboard said. "You coming or not?"

I raised my chin an inch. "Absolutely. Lead the way."

This wasn't my first gig with Tiffany's Temp Agency. I'd been doing short-term assignments for them for the better part of a year.

"What's the new job?" I asked as I followed the clipboard lady through a door and down a hallway.

"No idea." She stopped in front of the now-familiar red door that led to the interview room. "Tiffany Darnell wants to speak with you personally."

"Oh." My shoulders broadened. I'd never met the boss before. "Well, isn't *that* nice."

"Sure." She opened the door and motioned for me to enter. Inside, behind a sleek, glass-topped desk, sat a fiftyish, no-longer-quite-so-slim woman. She could've been my reflection in a mirror—if I'd had the budget for St. John Knits, Jimmy Choo shoes, and a fancy salon hairdo.

"Ms. Darnell?" I asked. "It's good to finally meet you."

"Ms. Fremden. Have a seat." Darnell nodded at the office chair in front of her desk. I took it.

As she studied the contents of a manila folder, I glanced around at the lavishly framed awards and degrees hanging neatly on the turquoise walls above her. I had a set at home just like them. A set of *one*, that is. A bachelor's degree in communications. I'd earned it back in the Late Crustacean Period.

"So, what job do you have for me today?" I asked, tucking an unruly lock of wavy, Clairol-medium-ash-brown hair behind my ear.

Darnell looked up from the papers in the folder. "First, I want to go over a few things from your last two jobs."

"Oh." I nodded. "Sure thing."

"Your stint at Sunken Gardens two weeks ago. Please explain. How did you manage to let an entire flock of Quaker parrots loose?"

I gulped. "Um ... You see, the lady in charge told me to fill the feeders in the parrot cage. *All by myself.*"

"So?"

"Did you know parrots have sharp talons? They can bite off your fingers with their beaks. I saw it on *Animal Planet*!"

Darnell's nose crinkled. "What are you talking about, Fremden?"

I fidgeted in my seat. "When I went in the cage, I could feel all those beady little eyes glaring at me! They were planning something, Ms. Darnell!"

"Planning? Planning what?"

"To attack me! Haven't you ever seen that Alfred Hitchcock movie, *The Birds*?"

Ms. Darnell closed her eyes and pinched the bridge of her nose. "Are you kidding me?"

"No! I'm telling you, those dirty little fiends were fixing to claw me to death and peck my eyes out! I freaked out and ran. I was afraid for my life!"

Darnell stared at me through her expensive bifocals until I flinched.

I shrunk back in my seat. "I guess you had to be there."

"No, Fremden, I *didn't*. That's what we hired *you* for. To be there. To do the jobs our clients pay us for!"

"But—"

She glared at me. Her lips puckered into a sparkly pink sphincter. "I'll have you know, your screw-up cost us that account."

I recoiled. "I'm sorry."

"Sorry doesn't pay the bills, Fremden. I'd planned to let this incident go. Then I got a call this morning about another one involving Melvin Flemster. What's all this about him firing you yesterday?"

I sat up and clutched my purse. "The man wanted me to compromise my principles!"

"At a pizza restaurant?" Darnell shook her head. "Mr. Flemster told me you refused to follow his explicit directions."

"The cheapskate wanted me to put four lousy little pepperoni slices on an extra-large pizza." I held up a handful of spread fingers for emphasis. "*Four*!"

Darnell frowned. "Wait. Flemster fired you for being too generous with the pizza toppings?"

"Not exactly." I glanced down at my lap. "He fired me because I wouldn't let *him* be too generous with my pizza *bottom*, if you catch my drift."

"What!" Ms. Darnell slammed a fist on the desk. "That's totally unacceptable!"

I nodded emphatically. "Exactly! That's why I grabbed my purse and left!"

"Hold on. You walked out? Why was I told he fired you?"

I bit my lower lip. "Well, on my way out, he did—after I kind of hit him over the head with a pizza pan."

"Geez, Louise, Fremden! That's *also* totally unacceptable!"

I shrugged. "What else was I supposed to—"

Darnell shoved an open palm in my face. "Save it. Look. I empathize with you, Fremden. I really do. But it's your word against his. Flemster's got a lump on his forehead the size of a walnut. What have you got to prove *your* side of the story?"

"My dignity, that's what!" I drew myself up to full sitting height. "You can't put a price on that!"

"Unfortunately, I can." Darnell tapped a manicured nail on her desk. "Flemster's attorney called this morning. Your dignity is going to cost us your week's wages and a personal apology. Otherwise, he's going to sue the agency for assault."

I crumpled. "Oh, crap. I'm sorry, Ms. Darnell. I ... I won't let it happen again."

"No, you won't." She slammed the manila folder closed. I saw my name written on the front of it, circled in red. "Part of the agreement with Flemster is that I have to let you go."

My mouth fell open. "What? Why?"

"To quote Flemster, 'So you can no longer be a menace to society at large.'"

I stood, outraged. "You're going to let that lecherous dirtbag win?"

"If it was just him, I'd say no. But word's gotten around, Fremden. No one wants to take you on as a temp anymore."

"But I'm *The Closer*!"

Darnell's perfect eyebrows met her perfect hairline. "You *know* about that?"

"Of course! You all call me The Closer because you can count on me to always close the job interview."

"Um ... Fremden? We call you The Closer because after you go to work for a company, they generally close their doors."

I blanched. "What?"

"They go *out of business*. Fremden, you're the retail version of the Grim Reaper. Apparently, your very presence causes cash registers to stop ringing and shop doors to shutter. Nobody wants to hire you. None of the clients from *my* agency, anyway."

My gut flopped. "What are you saying?"

Darnell tossed my folder into the wastebasket beside her desk. "I'm going to have to let you go. And *not* on a temporary basis."

"But ... what am I supposed to do *now*?"

She shrugged. "Take stock of your assets, I suppose."

I frowned. "What if I don't *have* any assets?"

"Well, I guess you can't bend over and kiss them goodbye then, can you?"

• • • •

BLINDSIDED FROM GETTING sacked by Ms. Darnell, I stumbled out of the cool orderliness of Tiffany's Temp Agency and into the sweltering chaos that was Florida in August. Instantly, my sunglasses fogged up and my clothes went limp.

Natives like me knew the dangers wrought by Florida's summer weather all too well. If a body couldn't secure an air-conditioned oasis within ten minutes of leaving the last one, the merciless sun would fry our brains to useless mush like a toad-frog in a microwave.

I mean, how else could you explain the bizarre crap-show that was Florida?

With only six minutes left until gray-matter meltdown, I made a mad dash for my car. Sweat was pouring off my temples when I hopped in and turned the ignition on Shabby Maggie, my 1963½ Ford Falcon Sprint convertible. She was a little older than me, but at the moment, I was the one feeling worse for wear.

I flipped the switch on the post-factory AC unit under the dash and held my arms up like wet cormorant wings so my sweaty pits could dry. I couldn't afford to stain the blue silk blouse I was wearing. For four years, it had been the top half of my go-to outfit. The bottom half had been forced to change along with the size of my thighs.

I wiped my brow and checked the gas tank. Being handed a pink slip instead of a paycheck meant Shabby Maggie wasn't the only one running on empty. I crossed my fingers. If I was lucky, I'd have enough fuel left to make it home. I shifted into drive and hoped for the best.

• • • •

HOW CAN IT BE THAT I'm almost 51 and I have pretty much zero *to show for my life?*

That was the question I pondered as I cruised down Gulf Boulevard past the beachside mom-and-pop motels baking in the sun like pastel candy boxes. I loved my hometown of St. Pete Beach. But if I didn't start bringing home the bacon, I'd have to trade in my tiny house on the Intracoastal for a trailer by the interstate.

How did my life get so far out of whack?

In my younger days, I'd been hardworking. Ambitious, even. So much so, that I'd saved up quite a decent clutch of nest eggs. My downfall had been putting them all in one basket. Well, *three* actually.

I'd gotten married and divorced. *Three times!*

The first didn't last a year. I called it my "Baptist starter marriage." The second one had lasted a lot longer, and the split had been amicable. The third time, not so much. Before I knew what was happening, my third ex had blown through my life savings on online poker and porn. Let me tell you, that's the kind of thing that can really take the starch out of a gal's sails.

My third divorce had been finalized four years ago. I'd tried my hand at numerous jobs since then, but no matter how hard I'd tried, I just couldn't find a toehold back onto the ladder of success. Starting menopause hadn't helped, either. I was rapidly losing the ability to muster up the energy to get out of bed, much less to be somebody's shiny new employee of the month.

Middle age had truly left me stuck in the middle. Unlike those perky women back at Tiffany's Temp Agency, I was no longer young and naïve enough to be enthusiastic about discovering an exciting new career—but I still wasn't old enough to kick back and collect Social Security. I also didn't possess the beauty required to become a trophy wife, yet I wasn't ugly enough to charge admission for a peek at the goods.

How was a gal like me supposed to make a living?

For the last year or so, I'd been limping along, making do with temporary jobs, walks on the beach, and gin. But getting fired from Tiffany's Temps was a wake-up call. I needed to find a job and a purpose for my life before I ended up living in my car at a truck stop on I-4.

I pulled up to a red light, my heart thrumming in my chest like a Phil Collins drum solo.

My life is a total disaster! What am I gonna do?

I closed my eyes and took a deep, calming breath.

Come on, Val. Life isn't so bad. You have friends. You have your health. You even have a decent boyfriend. And hey! Maggie's air conditioner is blowing like Frosty the Snowman in a hurricane. That's something, isn't it?

It was.

I gulped in a breath. Calmness swept over me.

Thank you, universe. Now, where do I go from here? Could you please give me a sign?

I opened my eyes and gasped. A gigantic naked man was staring down at me!

It was a sign, all right. A billboard, to be exact. On it was printed the image of a giant naked guy. Twenty feet of tan, muscular beefcake lay on a bed, staring at me with a come-hither look. The headline above his ripped torso read:

Never Wake Up Alone Again.

I dragged my eyes from his washboard abs toward the area of his, well, you know where. To my disappointment, a round, old-fashioned alarm clock had been strategically placed to hide his family jewels.

A speech bubble coming from the clock read:

"Mornin', Sweet Cheeks."

Something stirred inside my brain. My eyes shifted from the guy's clock-blocked manhood and back to his face. My mouth fell open. The man on the billboard was my old nemesis, Marco Shamway.

"You've got to be kidding me!" I screeched.

All through high school, that dirtbag had made my life a living hell. Teasing me in class. Taunting me in the halls. Driving my dorky, introverted self to skip lunch and hide out in the library with the other socially awkward nerds.

Marco had also headed the yearbook committee—the same one that had voted me "Most likely to become a Shoe Store Manager."

I winced. Over 30 years had come and gone since then, but the thought of being deemed worthy only to smell people's dirty feet for the rest of my life still stung like a flip-flop to the face.

I stared at Marco's flat stomach. The jerk didn't even have the human decency to get fat and ugly!

Then I spotted the caption at the bottom of the billboard.

The Hunk Clock. Just $29.99. Over 10 million sold!

A vein began to throb on my right temple. Rage boiled up inside me. I let loose a primal scream that could be heard in the next county.

"Aaargh!"

I was the one who'd come up with that whole Hunk Clock thing back in high school! I'd made it up as part of a short story assignment in English Lit—a class attended by Marco Shamway.

I could still remember how Marco had snatched the paper from my hand and read it out loud to his buddies. "Looks like Fremden's only boyfriend is gonna be a mechanical device," he'd teased. "Well, at least she found out early."

They'd laughed so hard I'd wanted to curl up and die.

I'd tried to push both Marco and the Hunk Clock out of my mind forever. But now, 30 years later, they were both back with a painful vengeance. While I sat here flat broke, that thieving scumbag Marco Shamway had stolen my idea and made millions off it—*instead of me!*

A horn honked behind me. The traffic light had turned green. I gritted my teeth and hit the gas. As I drove back toward my average little house to resume my below-average little existence, a very bad thought invaded my mind.

It was the kind of uncharitable thought that tended to fester away in a bubbling pot at the back of your mind. The kind of nasty notion you try to keep a tight lid on, and hope no one else finds out about.

I'm not saying it was the type of thought that could lead to murder ... but I wouldn't exactly rule it out, either.

Chapter Two

Every town had that one person. That seemingly ordinary guy or gal who, for some infuriatingly indiscernible reason, managed to rise from the depths of human obscurity and soar to fame and fortune like a god.

In my neck of the woods, the neighboring city of Clearwater had Hulk Hogan. St. Petersburg had Jack Kerouac. And, apparently, my little town of St. Pete Beach had Marco Shamway.

But it should've been *me*.

Red-faced and fuming mad, I pulled my old Ford into the cracked driveway of my tiny, concrete block house and slammed the brakes. I shoved the gear into park, yanked the keys from the ignition, and jerked open the door. As I hoisted myself from the seat, my shirt pocket caught on the doorframe and ripped.

"Seriously?" I yelled up at the sky, certain every demon-god ever born was laughing down at me from behind the clouds. "You've got to be kidding me!"

I slammed the car door and marched toward my front door. No amount of yoga or meditation was going to un-stink the trifecta of crap I'd just been slapped in the face with. This was a job for gin—and lots of it. If I'd had a swimming pool, I'd have filled it with Tanqueray and dived in.

I stormed into the house, threw my purse on the kitchen counter, and flung open the fridge. Given my budget, pickings were slim. Staring back at me were a quarter stick of butter and a piece of moldy cheese the color of mildewed moss.

Mercifully, on the top shelf were also half a lime and a liter bottle of store-brand tonic water. I grabbed them, set them on the counter, then reached into the freezer for the Tanqueray. There wasn't much left in the bright green bottle.

Hopefully it would be enough to save me from committing hari-kari. Or homicide.

Still boiling mad, I slap-dashed together a drink and swigged half of it down. Then I stomped into the living room and flopped onto the couch. My mind churned with fury.

Life is so unfair! I've already been screwed over twice. And now Marco Shamway? I've gotta find a way to get even with him!

I took another gulp of gin and tonic. My resolve slumped a notch.

Who am I kidding? I'm no match for him.

Even in high school, Marco had stood head and shoulders above the sea of average schleps like me. He was handsome, charismatic, and born with a silver spoon in his mouth. I, on the other hand, arrived on this planet mousy, forgettable, and fated to eat most of my meals alone with a plastic spork.

That insidious billboard flashed across my mind again. I gritted my teeth and took another slug from my glass.

I was certain that growing up, Marco had a nanny, a housekeeper, and a tutor. Being poor, both of my parents had had to work. I'd pretty much raised myself on a steady diet of Hamburger Helper, Nancy Drew mysteries, and after-school reruns. How was I supposed to know that Lucy and Ethel were never meant to be role models?

I stomped to the kitchen and made another drink, using up the rest of the Tanqueray. As I picked up the last wedge of lime, I envisioned Marco Shamway's smarmy face. I squeezed the lime so hard it shot across the kitchen and under the stove.

Argh! I bet this kind of crap never happens to Marco. So why does it always happen to me?

Marco had been the bane of my teenage existence. After graduation, I thought I'd never see his arrogant face again. But like so many things in my life, I'd been wrong about that, too. Marco was back, advertising his arrival on a freaking billboard, no less. Had he returned just to mock my mediocre, middle-aged existence?

Geez! What did I do to deserve this?

As I slugged back another mouthful of gin and tonic, I noticed the message light blinking on the old landline phone I kept around for emergencies—because in Florida, there were *always* emergencies.

Between lightning storms, monsoon rains, and hurricanes, the cell-phone towers around my area took a regular beating. But usually, I could count on the landline to still work for 9-1-1 calls, telemarketers, old friends who'd also lost cell coverage, and, of course, my boyfriend Tom Foreman.

"Ha!" I yelled, then shook my finger at an invisible Marco. "I bet you don't have a boyfriend as good as Tom!"

I grinned smugly at imaginary Marco and flopped back onto the couch. Good old Tom. I could always count on him.

At the moment, my boyfriend was pretty much the only thing working in my life—both literally and figuratively. Tall, blond, and built like a weightlifter, Tom was also handsome, smart, and a clean-freak. A lieutenant on the St. Petersburg police force, he'd been my boyfriend for the past four years. For a pig, that man could really bring home the bacon—and then fry me up in the sack.

I'd met Tom while I was trying to track down the heir to an old woman's will. Why he'd asked me out in the first place, I had no idea. Why he was still with me was an even bigger mystery. Secretly, I theorized that Tom must've suffered some kind of brain injury. The way I saw it, it was only a matter of time before his damaged synapses would reconnect. When they eventually did, he'd take one look at me and flee for his life.

I raised my drink to the empty room. "Here's to brain damage." I drained my glass, then punched the flashing red button on the message machine.

"Val? Hey. It's Tom. I ... um ... kind of got this special assignment. I can't talk about it right now. I'll tell you more later. But I wanted you to know I won't be home tonight. Or maybe for the next few days. Don't call me. I'll call you. Okay. Gotta go."

And then, in the background, right before the *click*, I heard a woman laugh.

Chapter Three

Someone was knocking on my front door.

A tad tipsy, I was sprawled out on my couch in the living room, just a few feet from the door. I scowled. Who the heck comes to your house unannounced nowadays? Only Mormons and sketchy kids selling magazine subscriptions, that's who.

No thanks.

As I glowered at the front door, the knock came again. Louder this time. I was about to yell, "Go away!" when whoever was out there *tried the doorknob*!

I bolted upright. Was there a thief out there casing my place? I hurried to the front window and took a cautious peek between the miniblinds.

A chunky man in expensive-looking clothes was walking away. He headed down my driveway toward a fancy red sports car parked in the street.

Who the heck is that? Wait! Could he be the Publisher's Clearinghouse guy?

I rolled my eyes.

With my luck? No way. Besides, I didn't even enter.

Given the day I was having, I figured it could only be bad news. I waited until I heard the roar of a car engine starting. Then I dared another peek between the slats in the blinds.

Whoever the guy was, he was driving a freaking Ferrari! I wracked my groggy brain.

Who do I know that can afford a Ferrari?

Nobody. Except Marco Shamway ...

But what reason would that jerk have to bother with the likes of me? Unless maybe he was worried that I'd sue him for stealing my idea. Had he sent one of his minions to dissuade me from pursuing damages? Or worse yet, kill me before I had a chance to tell anybody?

I thought about those murderous parrots at Sunken Gardens and grimaced. Maybe I was being a bit paranoid ...

I peeked between the blinds again and nearly swallowed my tonsils. The Ferrari was back! Whoever was driving it must've seen me. I stared, transfixed, my heart pounding in my chest. The car door opened. Whoever climbed out was wearing a ball cap pulled low. I couldn't see the top half of his face. But as he approached, I saw the man's mouth. It was a hard, determined line. The grimace of a man on a mission.

A mission to kill me.

This can't be happening! I don't want to die this way! I've got nothing interesting to put in my obituary!

• • • •

IT'S EXTRAORDINARY how the human mind switches to autopilot when one's life is at stake. Fight or flight, they call it. Survival mode. It's turned on by the primitive reptilian portion of our brains. Let me tell you, the moment that menacing man in the ball cap reached my front porch, my lizard brain kicked in, big time.

At first, I stood frozen in my tracks as the stranger tried my front doorknob again. Then, in an instant, I let go of the blinds and skittered and bounced through my house like a deranged albatross.

Like any wild animal, I was in search of an escape route. I knew instinctively that I couldn't exactly stand beside the sliding glass doors to the backyard. What if he walked around the house and saw me? So I ran to the only other room with a door leading outside—the garage.

I flew inside, slammed the door behind me, and immediately broke into a sweat from head to toe. Was it from fear or the sweltering heat? I couldn't tell. All I knew was that perspiration began pouring down my face as my untethered mind scratched and clawed and twisted inside my skull like a cat caught in a tornado.

I held my breath and blinked against the salty sweat stinging my eyes. Panic shot through me. Knees knocking, I flicked off the garage light and pressed my back against the dingy concrete wall for support.

The torn pocket on my blue silk blouse pulsed in rhythm to my wildly beating heart. I panted in the stifling heat. My hot, ragged breaths sucked in the familiar smells of motor oil and desperation.

Suddenly, I heard the roar of an engine starting. I nearly crumpled to the floor with relief. Then, to my utter horror, someone tried the handle on the roll-up garage door.

Oh, no! Please, oh please, let it be locked!

I slid down the wall and crouched in the corner. I tried to think of what to do next, but it was no use. Logic abandoned me. Overcome by a combination of booze, heat, and gas fumes, I blacked out.

Chapter Four

I awoke lying on the garage floor in a puddle of warm liquid. I touched the dark pool with a fingertip and held it to my nose. It had leaked out of me, all right. But it wasn't blood, sweat, *or* tears. My bladder had failed me.

How long have I been out?

Cautiously, I peeked around, then slowly sat up. Using an old rag beside me, I wiped the sweat from my face and strained to see in the dim, grayish light. I was still alive. But was I alone? Or was that guy in the ball cap hiding in here with me, waiting for me to regain consciousness?

I spied a hammer lying on a metal shelf next to me. I grabbed it. The feel of the handle in my hand instantly focused my mind and steeled my nerves.

Swallowing hard against the rising knot in my throat, I whispered into the dark. "Mister? If you're still in here, it's all good. We can talk this out."

There was no reply.

Keeping my back to the wall, I stood and licked the sweat from my upper lip. My eyes strained to survey the shadowy garage. It appeared to be empty. Then my eyes narrowed in on a dark figure lurking in a corner by the door.

My heart skipped a beat. The arrogant smile on his face was identical to the one Marco had sported on that infuriating billboard.

Steeling my nerves, I gripped the hammer with both hands and raised it over my head. Then I let out a screech that could curdle tapioca pudding and ran toward Marco like a psychotic ninja assassin. Before he knew what was happening, I sent the hammer crashing down, cracking his insipid skull in half.

"Ha! That'll teach you to mess with me!" I yelled.

As I stared down at his fractured skull, on some level, I knew what I'd done was wrong. I'm not trying to justify my actions, but seriously. Anyone with half a brain who'd managed to live past the age of 30 walked around harboring an indecent amount of pent-up rage inside them, didn't they?

The trick wasn't to *deny* it, but to find a "healthy release" for it. Right?

Right?

Some folks vented their psychotic thoughts by leaving nasty posts on social media. Others binged carbs by the mouthful. Still others popped edibles like candy.

As for me? I smashed ugly figurines to dust with my mighty "Hammer of Justice." If that was wrong, well, I didn't want to be right. And at this very moment, murderizing a figurine that kind of looked like Marco Shamway felt very right, indeed.

"So you thought I should manage a shoe store, did you?" I hissed at the broken statuette.

Marco's shiny ceramic eyes glinted up at me from either side of the jagged crack now separating them an extra quarter of an inch.

An evil smirk curled my lips. "What was that, Marco? You stole my Hunk Clock idea and thought you could get away with it? I don't think so!"

My Hammer of Justice came down again, shattering Marco's moronic clay head into a shower of chalky white confetti. Endorphins buzzed through me like a shot of warm heroin.

"Val? Is that you?" a woman's voice rang out from the other side of my garage door.

"Huh?" Ripped from my one-woman vengeance crusade, I blanched and nearly dropped my hammer.

My eyes darted around wildly at the ceramic shards littering the garage floor. Like Poe's beating heart hidden under the floorboard, these were the telltale remnants of a woman gone off her rocker.

Holy crap. How am I gonna explain this?

Up to now, I'd been able to hide my special brand of nutso from the general populace. But the broom and dustpan were both well out of reach in the kitchen. There was no way I could cover my crazy this time.

"Val? Are you in there?" the voice called out again. It belonged to my next-door neighbor, Laverne Cowens.

On the really short list of people who "got me," Laverne was right up at the top. In the five years I'd known her, the old woman had always accepted me just as I was—even when I'd found it hard to do so myself.

Maybe Laverne's former life as a Las Vegas showgirl had blurred her concept of what qualified as normal human behavior.

Or maybe she was a little cray-cray too, just like me.

Good lord, I could only hope.

Chapter Five

"**Y**oo-hoo. Val? I can hear you breathing in there!"

Until then, I hadn't noticed I'd been panting like a cougar in heat. For a woman her age, Laverne Cowens had uncanny hearing. I yanked up the rolling door and shot my seventy-something neighbor a sheepish smile.

"Hi, Laverne."

"Hiya, Honey! Who were you talking to?" Standing six-feet-two in gold high heels, Laverne's tobacco-tan visage towered over me like a mutant praying mantis.

"Uh ... nobody," I said.

"Nobody?" Laverne cocked her narrow, horsey head and glanced around the garage. Her wandering gaze narrowed in on the hammer in my hand, then shifted to the pulverized pile of porcelain in the corner. She raised a drawn-on eyebrow. "Does Tom know you're off the hammer wagon?"

A twinge of guilt shot through me. I groaned. "It's been the day from hell, Laverne. I got fired. I didn't get paid. Tom may be cheating on me. And if all that wasn't bad enough, on my way home I found Marco Shamway stole a fortune from me!"

Laverne's brow furrowed. She scratched a spot behind her ear with a red-lacquered fingernail. "Marco?"

I shifted on one foot. "High-school bully. The guy made my childhood miserable. And now he's gone and stolen a fortune that should've been mine!"

Laverne's right eyebrow rose to meet her left, forming a silvery McDonald's logo on her furrowed forehead. "Wow. That's a lot, Val."

I blew out a sigh. "Tell me about it."

"Hand over the hammer, Hun." Laverne reached out and gently pried it from my hand. The crack of her boney knees echoed through the dank garage as she squatted down to study Marco's pulverized plaster effigy.

I pouted. "Believe me, he had it coming, Laverne."

"Sure sounds like it."

Suddenly, Laverne's right arm flew up, then down, sending my Hammer of Justice crashing into Marco's crumbled remains. "Take that, you dirty scumbag!" she said, delivering a perfect bullseye to what was left of Marco's ceramic crotch.

As I stood there stunned, Laverne looked up and shot me a sympathetic smile. Then she rose to her full height like an overgrown grasshopper in a pink pantsuit. She handed me back the hammer. "Gee. That felt really good, Val."

I shot her a junkie's conspiratorial smile. "I know, right?"

She dusted off her hands. "Aww. And you tore your favorite blouse, too. How'd that happen?"

I glanced at my ripped pocket and shrugged. "Long story."

"And the pee-pants?"

I grimaced. "Even longer."

Laverne nodded. "I get it. The struggle is real. Even at my age, I'm not ready for Depends."

"It's not—" I gave up explaining, took the hammer from her hand, and set it back on the shelf. "Well, I guess I better go get cleaned up."

"Oh, sure." Laverne turned to go, then turned back toward me. She fished something from her shirt pocket. "I almost forgot. I found this tucked into your front door."

It was the business card of Anthony Bardsmore, Esq. The attorney had written a message on the bottom edge.

I need to speak to Val Fremden. It's a matter of urgency.

"This must be from the guy in the red Ferrari," I said absently.

"Red Ferrari!" Laverne gushed. "Did I ever tell you about the time Elvis drove me around in his pink Cadillac? Oh, it was so much fun!"

"Really?"

"You're darn tootin'!" She poked a finger at the card in my hand. "Hey! Maybe this guy wants to take *you* for a ride, too!"

I grimaced. "Geez. I sure hope not."

Chapter Six

After Laverne left, I reread the message scrawled at the bottom of Anthony Bardsmore's business card. The guy might not be a hired assassin. But he was a lawyer. And in my book, that was the same thing.

> *I need to speak to Val Fremden. It's a matter of urgency.*

My gut flopped.

Urgency was never good. What could be so urgent that a lawyer would be knocking at my door? That could only mean a summons—or I was being served.

OMG! Is Tom serving me with divorce papers so he can marry that woman on the voicemail? Was that what he'd meant when he said he was on "special assignment"?

I grabbed my cell phone and punched #7, his speed-dial number. It went directly to voicemail. I was about to give him a piece of my mind when I realized I didn't have any left to give.

What am I thinking? Tom can't divorce me. We aren't married!

I clicked off the phone and chewed my lip. If it wasn't Tom, then who? That blasted pizza guy Melvin Flemster? Was he suing me for assault?

I thought back to my conversation with Ms. Darnell at Tiffany's Temps. Was I supposed to apologize to Flemster, or was she? As far as I could remember, she hadn't made that point clear while she was canning me.

Then there was a third possibility. Maybe Bardsmore was representing Marco Shamway. If so, forget him! He'd already taken my idea. What else could he possibly want from me? What was left of my sanity? Well, good luck with that.

I set my cell phone down and drummed my nails on the kitchen counter.

Should I call this Bardsmore guy? Or should I get my own attorney first?

The only attorneys I knew were Laverne's husband J.D. Fellows, and an ambulance chaser named Ferrol Finkerman.

J.D. was retired. Plus he was up to his armpits moving into his new condo with Laverne. Ferrol Finkerman, on the other hand, probably had plenty of time on his hands—along with God knows what else. A mental image of him flashed in my mind. I grimaced.

Maybe I should call Morton & Morton. They have more billboards on the highway than Winkers & Yonder. That has to mean something, right?

I sighed and tossed the business card onto the counter. Suddenly exhausted, I sucked in a big breath. Instantly, I was overcome by a hideous odor. It smelled like sweat, urine, and broken dreams.

It was me.

"Pew!"

I wasn't sure how to proceed with Bardsmore. But my first order of business was crystal clear. I needed a long, hot, soapy shower. After that? I just might burn my entire outfit in the barbeque pit out back.

Chapter Seven

Not much goes unnoticed in my scruffy little neighborhood of Bahia Shores. It's full of snoops. Laverne was one, but not the worst. That honor went to Nancy Meyers who lived across the street. Her lemon-yellow Volkswagen wasn't in her driveway, so I seized the opportunity to walk to the road and check my mail unmolested by her prying eyes.

As I reached for the mailbox handle, I remembered a story I'd seen on the news the other day. A woman a few streets over had baked an actual loaf of bread inside her mailbox last week. Well, I had no desire to become the next news story at eleven; *Lady fries fingers off on mailbox handle.*

I gave the mailbox a quick karate chop. It fell open. Inside the steaming box I found the usual assortment of pre-heated bills. But along with them was something else. A box about the size of half a loaf of bread. It had been wrapped in brown paper, and on it someone had written the words:

Don't open until the big day!

"What you got there?" a voice called out.

Startled, I looked up. Laverne was kneeling in her front yard, waving a gloved hand at me. I hadn't noticed her pulling weeds around her garden bed inhabited by a few scrawny palms and an impressive collection of garden gnomes.

"Oh. Hey, Laverne." I shook the box. "I'm not sure. Some kind of gift, I think."

"Oh! I've got one for you, too!"

"You do?"

"Yes! I'll go get it."

"How about you come over for a drink?" I called out. Fresh from the shower, perspiration was already beading on my upper lip. I didn't want to spoil my fresh t-shirt and shorts. "I'll leave the door open for you."

"Sure, thing, Honey! See you in a minute."

As I passed Shabby Maggie on my way back into the house, I tossed the package onto the passenger seat. I wasn't sure what "the big day" was, but it certainly wasn't today. There was one thing I knew for sure, though. If I took that thing inside, I couldn't be trusted not to open it.

• • • •

I POURED THE HOT BREWED tea into a pitcher of cool water and waited on Laverne. When I'd inherited my little house five years ago, the unflappable former showgirl had come along as part of the package.

I'd slowly come to appreciate the ditzy septuagenarian's puppy-dog loyalty. She was always ready to help, and to dole out her unique brand of odd, yet often eerily accurate advice—the kind you just don't find any more in today's politically correct society.

Since I tended to lean more toward the pessimistic side, Laverne's unsinkable cheerfulness had taken some getting used to. And to be honest, sometimes the things she said still made me wince like a flashlight to the face in the middle of the night.

But as I let her in the front door, I felt a twinge of sadness. I knew our chummy camaraderie was about to come to an end. Laverne had recently remarried. In a few days, she'd be moving into a fancy condo downtown with her husband, J.D. The mere thought of it made me want to go back into the garage and give Marco another whack.

"So, what are you gonna tell Tom?" Laverne asked, walking up to the kitchen counter and plopping onto a barstool.

I cringed, then poured the tea into two glasses of ice and handed her one. "Why do I have to tell Tom about the figurine? It only cost 50 cents at a yard sale."

34

The way I saw it, pulverizing hideous figurines to dust was a public service—and a whole lot cheaper than psychotherapy.

Laverne set her glass on the counter. "I'm not talking about *that*, Val. I'm talking about you losing your job again. What's this make? Four jobs in two months?"

"Five. If you count Melvin Flemster." I flopped onto the barstool next to Laverne. "What's wrong with me? Am I some kind of weirdo loser?"

Laverne laid a boney hand on my shoulder. "You aren't a loser, Honey. You just haven't found your true inspiration yet."

I frowned. "My *true inspiration*?"

"Of course!" Laverne smiled softly. A faraway look clouded her big doe eyes. "Not many people know this, but I used to wear a thong bikini and sell hotdogs from a cart on Fremont Street in Vegas. You know, before they put that big dome thingy over it and all."

"Really?" I said, surprised.

Laverne laughed. "Really." She shook her head. "I thought I'd be working that wiener wagon till the day I died. But then a miracle happened."

I blanched. "A *miracle*?"

"You better believe it! One day a gorgeous woman appeared in front of me like a mirage, Val! I'll never forget it. She was wearing a pink sequined bodysuit and had a humongous plume of white feathers in her hair. That angel changed my life."

Laverne stared up at the ceiling, as if a movie of her close encounter with Our Lady of the Wiener Wagon was playing on the plaster above our heads. If it was, *I* couldn't see it. I waited as long as my natural impatience would allow, then asked, "So, what happened?"

Laverne shifted her gaze toward me. "Why, she ordered a foot-long Showdog with mustard and extra relish!"

I blew out a breath. "A true miracle indeed."

Laverne cocked her narrow head. "Don't be silly, Val. *That's* not what changed my life."

"I would certainly *hope* not. Let me guess. She left you a big tip?"

"Why, yes!" Laverne gushed. "That beautiful lady also gave me a pass to her nightclub act. I'm telling you, the second I saw her on stage, *bam*! I knew I wanted to be a showgirl, just like Bambi Bardoobie."

Seriously? I hope that's a stage name.

"How did you *know* you knew?" I asked.

The skinny old woman shot me a motherly smile. "I can't say exactly. It was like ... a beam of light hit me." She sighed dreamily. "I didn't choose *it*, Val. *It* chose *me*."

I scowled. "Are you saying your whole life was transformed by some chance meeting with a bimbo?"

Laverne's smooth, unworried brow remained un-creased. "Not *bimbo*, Val. *Bambi*."

I stifled an eye roll. "I stand corrected."

Laverne shook her head softly and glanced up at that imaginary movie on the ceiling again. "Wow. That was 50 years ago. But it seems like only yesterday."

I groaned. "*Fifty years* ago? That's as long as I've been *alive*, Laverne. And let me tell you, I've *never* felt that certain about *anything. Ever!*"

Laverne's round, pug eyes shifted from the ceiling back down to me. "You will one day, Hun. Just keep trying."

"I *have* been. But I keep *failing*."

Laverne's face registered shock and surprise. "Val! You aren't failing. You're *learning*."

"Learning what? About what a big loser I am?"

"No!" Laverne set her glass of tea on the counter. "Honey, you're learning about what kind of big loser you *don't* want to be."

My nose crinkled. "Huh?"

"Sure! Some people know what they want to be right off the bat. For other folks, it's more like a process of elimination. Don't you know that by now?"

Apparently not.

I pouted grumpily. "I'm still not following you."

Laverne patted my hand. "Okay. Let's start with the jobs you've had. What you liked and didn't like about them."

"Uh ... okay."

"So, tell me, Honey: what was wrong with working at that accounting firm with your friend Milly?"

I cringed. Working at Griffiths & Maas had been my longest-lasting employment stint since coming back to St. Pete Beach. I'd toughed it out almost six months—mainly for the sake of my friend, Milly Halbert. After that, well, I'd gone through more odd jobs than I cared to remember.

My upper lip snarled. "One word, Laverne. *Accounting.*"

Laverne nodded and sighed. "I'll give you that one. So, what about that job at that fancy hotel?"

"As a bed warmer?" My face puckered with disgust. "They made me wear a full hazmat suit to get under the sheets. Like I was some flea-ridden mutt that might contaminate the place! Just so some rich guy didn't have to warm his own bed at night? It was degrading!"

Laverne pursed her lips and nodded slowly, like an indulgent psychoanalyst. "And that job standing in line to buy tickets and stuff for people?"

"No good. Neither my feet nor my patience have the stamina for that kind of crap anymore."

"I get that, too, Honey. So, what about handing out coupons for Winnie and Winky's donut shop?"

I winced at the memory. "I dunno, Laverne. Is it just me, or is the general public not quite the same caliber it used to be?"

Laverne shook her head and looked away wistfully. "No. It's not just you, Honey."

I was about to throw in the towel when Laverne's head suddenly spun back around. She grinned, grabbed my hand, and gave it a hard squeeze. "Val, I've got it!"

"Got what?"

Laverne beamed her pearly dentures at me. "Your dream job description, of course!"

My mouth fell open. "You do?"

"Uh-huh. Val, what you need is a job where you don't have to do math, wear a hazmat suit, have patience, or interact with your fellow man!"

The old woman's simple genius caused a realization to switch on in my head. I was an incorrigible grump. "Geez, Laverne. Is there such a job as Curmudgeon for Hire?"

Laverne squirmed with excitement and picked up her cell phone. "I don't know. Let's check on Craigslist!"

I sighed. "I meant that as a joke."

"Oh." Laverne's shoulders slumped for a moment, then her eyes grew bright. "Hold on a second. Are you still taking that writing course?"

I winced. "Yeah. So?"

"Does writing require math or any of those other things you hate?"

I thought about it for a second. "Uh ... not generally, no."

"Well, then, problem solved, Honey! You can be a writer!"

"Oh, sure. Because that's such an easy field to make a fortune with."

Laverne's face was lit up. "So, it's perfect!"

I forced a smile so as not to disappoint my friend. But the idea of me becoming a writer was already dead in the water. A couple of weeks ago, I'd submitted an article to the local tabloid, the *Beach Gazette*. I'd never heard anything back.

"But what if this writing idea doesn't pan out?" I asked.

Laverne shrugged. "Then something *else* will. Val, you're not a loser. You're just a late bloomer."

"Late bloomer?" I scoffed. "I'm about to turn 51, Laverne. If I wait any later, I'll be 'blooming' into my diapers in a nursing home."

"Oh! Oh!" Laverne squirmed on her barstool like an elementary school kid with the right answer. "I know! I've got a job for you right now!"

"You do?"

"Yes! You can help *me*. I need to take some junk to the thrift store!"

I smirked. "Now *that* sounds like a job with real career potential. What's the pay?"

"Five bucks. Cash money!"

"Tempting, but you don't have to pay me."

"Yes, I do. And how about I throw in a donut stop on the way back?"

I glanced down at the crumpled newspaper on the kitchen counter. Circled in red was the only classified ad I thought I might qualify for. It was a part-time position as a pet-food taster.

Hmm. Donuts or dog food?

I pushed the paper away. "Okay. I'm in. When do we start?"

Laverne grinned. "There's no time like the present!"

I shrugged, then remembered something. "Wait. Speaking of presents, I thought you were going to bring me one."

Laverne grinned. "I just *did*, silly. It's a trip to the thrift store. You can pick out anything you like!"

Oh, boy. I can't wait.

Chapter Eight

My home state of Florida was a mecca for birds.

Everywhere you looked you could spot odd ducks, loons, dodos, and vultures. But no matter the species, you could bet your bottom dollar most of these misfit creatures had flapped down to the Sunshine State for the same reason: to escape the mess of a nest they'd left behind back home.

Snowbirds supposedly migrated here to avoid the winter cold. Waders came to shuffle along the shorelines in search of the "beach life," whatever *that* was. Anybody with a TV knew jailbirds took flight from the law here by the thousands. In fact, Florida was chock-a-block with birdbrains on the wing, attempting to evade taxes, exes, indictments, alimony, child support, and other bothersome societal obligations.

But given the sheer number of old geezers flocking around St. Pete Beach, I was pretty sure they'd flown down here in an attempt to outrun death itself. At the moment, even my neighbor Laverne was trying to dodge a potentially deadly bullet of her own.

As she and I stood inside her immaculate single-car garage, I realized she was on the run from her new husband's ugly past ...

I picked up one of the thrift-store boxes destined for the trunk of her white Lincoln Continental. "Uh, Laverne? Why are all these boxes labeled J.D.?"

Laverne's nose crinkled at the sight of her husband's initials scrawled on the carton in black magic marker. "Uh ... they're all stuff of his that I can't stand."

I smirked. "No further explanation necessary."

Laverne and I were sisters of fate. Like me with my third husband, Laverne had gone and fallen for a man of German heritage. I'd barely survived divorcing mine. Laverne, on the other hand, was just beginning to realize the seriousness of the situation she'd gotten herself into.

After retiring from his law practice last year, J.D. had begun moving his stuff into Laverne's home. Over that time, I'd witnessed her colorful collection of Vegas memorabilia—mainly festive celebrity bobble-heads and casino shot-glasses—be overrun by a silent, relentless army of dull-eyed Hummel figurines sporting ugly boots and party-pooper babushkas.

If that weren't bad enough, the walls of Laverne's home, once covered with kitschy velvet paintings of Elvis, Evel Knievel, Tom Jones, and Johnny Cash, had become infested with grainy, black-and-white pictures of dour-faced, beer-bellied men in lederhosen. Having lived with my boyfriend Tom for almost two years, I knew full well the whole cohabitation struggle was real.

I put the box in the trunk of her car and picked up another one. I shook it. Disappointingly, it made no noise. "Uh, Laverne, your marriage license isn't in one of these boxes, is it?"

Laverne raised a drawn-on eyebrow. "Gosh, no, Honey. I love J.D."

"Okay. Just checking."

I set the carton in the cavernous trunk of the Lincoln next to the first one, then picked up a third. I shook it, too. I was listening for the telltale *clink* of porcelain on porcelain.

Ever since I'd spotted J.D.'s collection of Hummel figurines in Laverne's house, my hammer hand had been twitching to smash the whole lot to smithereens. I couldn't help it. During my disastrous third marriage, I'd developed quite a penchant for what I called the *trifecta perfecta*: a hammer, a Heineken, and a Hummel. After a while, it had become an autonomous response.

While Laverne dug through her purse for her car keys, I covertly shook the last carton, listening for the distinctive sound given off by my favorite prey. If any of J.D.'s Hummels were lurking inside, I wanted first dibs.

But the last carton didn't clink either.

Drat.

I frowned and shoved the box into the trunk beside the other three. "So, where are we hauling his junk off to?"

"That thrift shop on Corey Avenue, if I can ever find my silly car keys."

As I closed the trunk, I noticed a set of keys dangling from the lock. I yanked them out. "These what you're looking for?"

Laverne stopped scrounging in her purse and looked up. "Oh. Thank goodness!" She snatched the keys from my hand. "Come on. We better get a move on!"

"What's the hurry?"

"The movers will be here first thing tomorrow morning." Laverne winked a big doe eye at me. "Hey. Can I help it if a few boxes get lost along the way?"

I laughed. "Absolutely not. That kind of crap happens *all* the time."

• • • •

ST. PETE BEACH LAY midway down a long strip island that hugged the western shore of Central Florida. Blessed with sugar-white sands and the normally calm, aqua waters of the Gulf of Mexico, it was a mecca for vacationers from around the world.

At the moment, Laverne and I were cruising north along Gulf Boulevard, the main drag running up the middle of the narrow island. With her at the wheel, I tried to let go of the anxiety gnawing at my gut. I had a lot on my mind—not the least of which was how much I was going to miss having Laverne living right next door.

But I couldn't change that. So, I resigned myself to a familiar amusement—watching the colorful parade of sunburned tourists stumbling down the sidewalks on their way to and from the kitschy shops and bars designed to pick their wallets clean.

I spotted an obviously drunk guy trying to get his fat foot back into his wayward flip-flop. I laughed and turned to Laverne. "What a beautiful day for a ride in a convertible. We should've taken Shabby Maggie."

"No, Honey. Not today."

"Why not?"

Laverne's usually smiling lips were a grim line as she steered the huge Lincoln right onto 75th Avenue. "I don't want to mess up my hair. J.D. and I have to meet with that blasted condo committee again this afternoon."

My nose crinkled. "Condo committee?"

"Yes. Those cranky old people at The Oversight. They make new residents jump through hoops like circus-trained Chihuahuas! I'm telling you, Val. I haven't been this nervous since I tried out for *A Chorus Line* at the Flamingo."

"Geez."

Laverne sighed. "I guess they don't want any weirdos living there."

I laughed. "Well, that rules out most of the people around here. So, what's the name of this place?"

"The Oversight. I thought I just said that."

"No. I meant the thrift store."

"Oh." Laverne frowned. "I can't remember exactly. Bella's, or something like that. It's not exactly catchy, like Caesar's Palace. But I remember it's right across from the movie theater."

I nodded. "Okay. I can work with that."

I sat back and tried to enjoy the ride, glad for the distraction from whatever impending disaster might befall me at the hands of attorney Anthony Bardsmore.

St. Pete itself was like a balm to my soul. I never got tired of the scenery. Palm trees. Turquoise water. Lobster-faced tourists. What wasn't to love? And I was lucky enough to own my own little piece of paradise here.

I gulped.

Unless Bardsmore was with the IRS and I somehow owed a boatload of back taxes I knew nothing about.

• • • •

BY THE TIME WE REACHED the bridge onto the mainland, I was frazzled with worry again. I was chewing my third fingernail when Laverne steered her shiny white Lincoln onto Corey Avenue. Instantly, the kitschy beach vibe changed, and we were staring at a scene from Mayberry RFD, circa the Great Depression.

Built back in the 1930s, the old Corey Avenue Business District had, in its heyday, been the shining star of the local area. Like me, however, its fortunes had sagged over the years. If we'd been in Arizona, I swear there'd have been tumbleweeds rolling down the sidewalks.

I leaned forward and stared out the windshield, trying to find the thrift shop amongst the shabby storefronts lining both sides of the street. Laverne and I cruised slowly by an old-timey hardware store, a couple of vacant window fronts, a dreary craft boutique, a miniscule coffee shop, a tarot and crystal store, and a dusty-looking antiques emporium.

Toward the end of the road on the left, I spotted what I was looking for. It was the towering Art-Deco marquee of the tiny Beach Theatre.

"The thrift shop must be right around here," I said.

Laverne tapped the brakes. We rolled slowly up to the tiny, one-screen movie theater. The most distinctive building on the whole block, the vintage marquee displayed the theater's current offering. It was *Paradise Lost.*

I sighed.

How apropos.

I glanced across the street. Just as Laverne had said, staring back at me with blank, plate-glass eyes was a sketchy junk shop with the oddest moniker I'd ever seen.

"Belated Rooms?" I read aloud. My nose crinkled. "Geez. What kind of weird name is that?"

Laverne shrugged. "How should I know? Oh! Did I ever tell you? I used to know a guy named Ben D. Over. He worked in a carnival sideshow."

At a loss as to how to respond to that, I simply smiled and nodded. Laverne maneuvered her sheet-metal battle cruiser into a parking spot near the thrift store's front door. When she shifted into park, I reached for the door handle.

"Wait!" Laverne squealed.

"What?"

She put a finger to her lips, then rolled down the window and glanced around.

"What are you looking for?"

"J.D.! You don't see his black Mercedes anywhere, do you?"

I scanned the street. "No. Looks like the coast is clear."

Laverne eyed me funny. "I know that Val. It's gorgeous out. But I can't go to the beach right now. The hair, remember?"

I sighed. Typical, ditzy Laverne. I was going to miss her so much.

"Of course," I said. "What was I thinking?"

Chapter Nine

The grimy glass door creaked like a rutting toad as I pushed it open and peeked inside. My nose crinkled at the pungent assault of stale grease, faded perfume, and unchecked body odor. Against my better judgment, I took a tentative step inside.

"Hello? Anybody here?" I called out.

Nobody answered.

"Did somebody die in here?" Laverne asked, stumbling in behind me waving a hand in front of her puckered face.

"If they did, how could you tell?" I asked. "Look around. This place is a dump!"

Crammed with the discarded detritus of lives unremarkably lived, Belated Rooms had that sketchy, neglected feel of one of those half-museum, half-junk places you find along the roadside in rural townships with no traffic lights.

"Hello?" I called out again, louder this time.

My voice echoed off the walls. Belated Rooms appeared to be as deserted as a post-apocalyptic garage sale.

"It smells like a dead scarecrow in here," Laverne said. "I don't want this stank to get on me, Val. Those old folks at The Oversight will flunk me for sure!"

I chewed my lip for a moment. "Maybe we should just dump the boxes and run."

Laverne nodded eagerly. "Yes! Let's do *that*."

She turned back toward the exit. I took a step to follow her. Suddenly, a crash sounded from somewhere amidst the heap of junk inside the thrift store.

Laverne locked eyes with me and squawked, "What was that?"

"Sounded to me like the crunch of galvanized steel against mass-produced Chinese porcelain," I said. "But I could be wrong."

"Jerry, you deadbeat! I'm gonna kill you!" a gravelly voice rang out from somewhere in the back of the shop.

"Kill?" Laverne gulped, her eyes bulging from her skull.

I grimaced. "Uh ... I think you're right, Laverne. Let's get the heck out of here." I yanked open the door, causing it to let out another randy-toad squeak.

"Who's there?" the mysterious voice yelled.

"Nobody!" Laverne yelped. "We were just leaving! We didn't hear anything about killing anyone! We swear!"

"Hold on!" the raspy voice barked.

Frozen in place like two dumb chicks in a horror flick, Laverne and I stared, wide-eyed, in the direction of our unknown potential axe murderer.

As we stood transfixed, from behind a cheap bookcase crammed with dime-store knick-knacks, the shriveled head of an elderly woman appeared. Her hair, dyed jet black some time ago, sported a three-inch-wide skunk stripe of gray roots.

"Y'all looking to buy or sell?" the woman asked as she walked toward us, dusting herself off as if she'd been lying amid a heap of fallen debris.

Laverne raised her hand. "Uh ... excuse me. How much does it cost to leave?"

The old woman laughed. "Too much for me, I suppose." She shook her head, sending a shower of either dust or dandruff onto the shoulders of her ratty blue T-shirt. "I've been chained to this place for two years without one single miserable vacation."

Laverne's pug eyes bulged. "And you just broke free?"

"Uh ... sorry to bother you," I said, stepping in front of Laverne. "We were just looking to unload a few boxes of unneeded merchandise. Do you want it?"

The woman studied me as she scratched a mole on her neck. "For free?"

I glanced at Laverne. She nodded like a bobble-head in an earthquake.

"Yes, for free," I said. "We were hoping you could just take the stuff off our hands."

The old woman slapped on a pair of lime-green bifocals and peered at us. "I'm not falling for that crap again. You two are gonna have to show me what you got first. I don't take roadkill."

"Uh ... sure." I glanced over at Laverne. "Okay with you?"

Laverne nodded. "I haven't dumped any dead animals since I broke up with Johnny Two-Fingers."

I blanched. "What?"

Laverne brushed my question away with a casual flick of her wrist. "That was ages ago. While I was working at that wiener wagon I told you about. You know, before Bambi Bardoobie made me see the light."

"Bambi Bardoobie?" the skunk-haired lady asked.

I winced. "It's a long—"

"The Vegas showgirl?" she spoke over me.

My mouth fell open.

"You know her?" Laverne asked. Her eyes, once fearful, now glowed as bright as new pennies.

"*Know* her?" The old woman scoffed. "We used to be *roommates*." She bent over and tugged up one leg of her grungy green polyester pants until it was up to her hairy knee.

I winced.

Dear lord. This can't be good ...

"Recognize these gams?" she asked.

Before I could muster a reply, the old lady kicked up her leg, raising her croc-sandaled foot as high as my head.

"Ha!" she laughed. "See? I still got it. I'm Geraldine Jiggles. Used to work at the Golden Nugget."

Laverne gasped. "I'm Leggy Lulu! Showgirl at the Showboat!"

The two old ladies sized each other up for a moment. Then, just like one of those weird courtship rituals you see on *Animal Planet*, Laverne mimicked Geraldine's odd performance. She yanked up her own polyester pant leg and kicked like a bucking mule.

Geraldine nodded appreciatively and rubbed the whiskers on her chin. "Looks like you still got it, too, Lulu."

"Thanks, Jiggles!" Laverne gushed.

Apparently satisfied with each other's outward display of vitality, the pair cackled with glee. Then the duo flung an arm around each other's shoulders and broke into an impromptu can-can, like a couple of crazy old loons paddling around on Swan Lake.

I know. If my life weren't already a ridiculous crap-show, I wouldn't have believed it either.

Chapter Ten

Reeling from being the hapless witness to a vaudeville act older than Abbott and Costello, I shook my head. Could my life get any more absurd?

While the two faded Vegas starlets swapped memories and rusty old routine moves, I slipped out the front door of Belated Rooms. I wasn't planning my escape. I had work to do. If I was going to earn my five bucks and a donut chaser, I needed to get busy hauling J.D.'s boxes out of Laverne's trunk and into the thrift shop.

As I fumbled back inside with the last of the four cartons, I heard Geraldine say, "And that's how I keep a leg up on the competition!" She cackled at Laverne, then slapped her polyester-clad thigh.

I stifled a groan.

Seriously? Well, at least I missed the comedy portion of the Geraldine Jiggles variety show.

"Okay, that's all of the boxes," I said.

"Thank you, Honey!" Laverne said.

Huffing from the heat and the effort, I swiped at the sweat trickling down my temples and looked around for a place to sit. I perched atop a wooden TV/stereo/turntable console from the 1970s. The dusty beast looked like a coffin built for a dead daybed. My keister planted, I leaned back against the wall and tried to cool off and catch my breath as I watched the unlikely pair get down to business.

"Humph," Geraldine grunted. She shuffled over to the boxes and began circling them like a homicidal hobo. "What is all this junk, Lulu?"

"My husband's stuff," Laverne said. She nodded eagerly at the boxes. "You do the honors, Jiggles."

"Okay. Let's see what you got." Geraldine pushed her lime-green bifocals higher up the bridge of her red nose.

Then she pulled a box cutter from her pants pocket. With a few grunts and groans, she got down on her knees and sliced through the blue tape sealing one of J.D.'s boxes.

I craned my neck for a peek at what was inside. But from my vantage point atop the TV console, all I could see was bubble wrap and skunk hair. I was about to hop off the thing when Geraldine did something so odd, I thought I'd better keep my distance.

She opened the box as if she thought it might detonate.

Leaning her torso back away from the carton as far as possible, Geraldine stretched her arms and cautiously lifted the flaps with the tips of her fingers. She cringed, waited a few beats, then bent forward over the box and took a deep whiff. "Huh. Smells all right."

"It's not a bomb," I said. "And it's not roadkill."

Geraldine glanced up at me. "Fine. But you'd be surprised what can crawl into a cardboard box and die, Missy. Or worse yet, *live*. One time, I opened a box like this and a dang *bat* came flying out! Then there was this other time—"

Geraldine's cell phone rang. She pulled it from her shirt pocket, glanced at the display, then looked up at Laverne. "Hold up a sec. I gotta get this." The old woman glanced over at me, tucked the box cutter back into her pocket, and wagged a nicotine-stained finger at both me and Laverne. "Don't you two go anywhere. You hear?"

"We won't," Laverne said. "We promise."

"Good." Geraldine heaved herself up off her knees with a mighty grunt, then shuffled in her pink crocs over to a u-shaped, Plexiglass showcase. Heaped with junk, the case apparently served as the shop's checkout counter, jewelry display, and used plastic-bag recycling station, to name a few.

Laverne glanced over at me and shrugged. Then her pug eyes darted left and right at the odd assortment of junk all around the shop. "Val, I'm gonna go look for a rain cap. I need to keep the smell of this place out of my hair. I just had a wash-n-set, for crying out loud!"

I patted the gigantic console I was still perched atop. "Knock yourself out. I'll be right here."

"You don't want to look around?"

"Nope. I'm good."

Truth be told, I was about to be very *bad*.

With Geraldine busy on the phone and Laverne browsing the store, I seized the opportunity I'd been hoping for. I was going to rifle through J.D.'s box and hopefully snag myself a Hummel figurine!

Keeping one ear on Geraldine's conversation and one eye on Laverne, I slipped off the console. Employing stealthy moves I'd seen on *The FBI Files*, I crouched down and crab-walked over to the open box. Soundlessly, I snatched off the top layer of bubble wrap. Underneath was an assortment of meticulously wrapped parcels. I grabbed one and unfurled the squishy bubble wrap. I nearly squealed with delight.

Jackpot! A Hummel!

I glanced around. No one had noticed. I grinned, crammed the figurine into the back waistband of my jeans, then scurried over to the entertainment console and plopped my butt back atop it. Proud of my smooth moves, I smirked and casually picked at my nails.

Hmm. I wonder if I still have a Heineken at home ...

"Uh-huh," Geraldine said from behind the yellowed plastic checkout cubicle. "Crap. Well, if you see him, have him call me A.S.A.P., okay? Thanks."

The old woman hung up, then punched in another number on her cell phone. She waited, sour-faced, as it must've rung and gone to voicemail. "Jerry? Pick up, for crying out loud! Where are you, you lazy scumbag?"

"Ugh!" Geraldine slammed her phone down on the counter. As she made her way past the heaps of junk and back over to me, ghosts of muttered curses tumbled from her lips.

"Sup?" I asked, trying to sound breezy.

Geraldine shot me a wary glance, then studied the box and sucked her teeth. "Something looks different."

"Yeah. I took off the first layer of bubble wrap for you. Just trying to be helpful."

Geraldine shot me a *yeah, right* look, then unwrapped one of the bundles. It was another Hummel. One even uglier than the one now suffocating face-down inside my underpants.

I squirmed with envy as Geraldine turned the Hummel over in her hands. Dollar signs danced in her eyes, then were quickly snuffed out. She looked me dead in the eye and yelled, "Hey, Lulu! This junk looks okay. I'll take it off your hands. No charge."

"You will?" Laverne asked from somewhere amidst the junk in the shop. She emerged from behind a pile of old clothes and came clattering up to us in her gold high heels. "Oh, you're a doll, Jiggles! Thanks for making it so easy!"

"Don't mention it." Geraldine frowned. "One problem solved. One to go." She turned and stared at me.

I felt my cheeks catch flame. "Uh ... what problem is that?"

Geraldine sighed. "I need to find somebody to help me out around here. That stupid Jerry. I never know from one day to the next if he's gonna show up or not."

Laverne cocked her head. "Jerry?"

"Yeah. Jerry Nokowski." Geraldine blew out a lungful of stale cigarette breath. "He was supposed to be here an hour ago already. If he doesn't show up by tomorrow morning, I may have to shut down the shop temporarily."

"Gee," I deadpanned. "How will the neighborhood survive?"

Geraldine glowered at me, then turned her attention to the Hummel in her hand and muttered, "I finally book myself three lousy days off and *this* happens. If Jerry doesn't show up for work, how am I gonna find a replacement before I leave tomorrow?"

Laverne gasped. Her eyes grew wide with delight. She locked those crazy eyes on me.

Oh, no. Laverne, no!

I grimaced and shook my head—but subtlety was never Laverne's forte.

"I know," Laverne blurted. "Why don't *you* do it, Val?"

My body went limp.

Aww, crap.

Geraldine turned her skunk-striped head my way and stared at me. "Well, what do you say?" she asked. "You free?"

"No, I'm not *free*," I grumbled. "I only work for pay."

Laverne gushed, "She just finished a position in retail last night. She's available right now!"

Unbelievably, Geraldine's ungrateful eyes narrowed with suspicion. "You got any references?"

Seriously?

I shrugged. "Nope. Not a *single* one."

Geraldine frowned. "Who was your last employer?"

"Melvin Flemster!" Laverne said.

Geraldine grimaced. "That creep from the Pizza Palace?"

I shot her with my finger gun. "That'd be the one."

Geraldine's expression shifted from suspicion to something bordering on respect. Either that, or she had indigestion. "If you can work for that guy, you can handle *anything*," she said.

I scooted my butt off the outdated console. "Gee, thanks."

Geraldine sidled up to me. "Uh ... what's your name again?"

I blew out a long, tired breath. "Val Fremden."

"Listen, Fremden. This job's a total no-brainer. All you need is basic math to run the register, a little patience for when business is slow, and of course, the ability to deal with the public."

I rolled my eyes. "You forgot the hazmat suit."

"Huh?"

"Nothing." I held up a blank palm. "Look. I'm flattered and all, but—"

"Go on, Val. Take the job!" Laverne squealed. "Jiggles, Val is an excellent employee. Reliable and trustworthy. Scouts' honor!"

Geraldine pursed her wrinkled lips. "So, you'll do it?"

"Uh ..." I started backing up toward the exit door. "I'll think about it, okay?"

"Well, don't think too long," Geraldine said, mirroring my backward escape attempt step for step like a tango dancer. "My plane leaves for Vegas tomorrow at one!"

Laverne clasped her hands together. "How exciting! How long will you be gone?"

"Three days. Four tops." Geraldine shoved a business card at me. "Come on, Fremden. I'll make it worth your while."

"Uh, right." I took the card with my right hand while the left one pushed open the front door. "Hurry up, Laverne!" I yelled over the toad-like squeak of the door hinges. "We've got to go. You've got that condo meeting, remember?"

"Oh! That's right!" she said. "But first, tell me. How do I look?" Laverne grinned and gestured to a ratty, yellow-polka-dot rain cap atop her head.

I winced. "Like you just survived an explosion at a plastic bag factory?"

Laverne beamed. "I'll take it!" She turned to Geraldine. "How much?"

"For you, Lulu? It's on the house."

"Your generosity knows no bounds," I said sourly. "Considering all the stuff Laverne just gave you, I don't know how you'll manage to turn a profit."

Geraldine shot me some side-eye. "You know what, Missy? I'll show you how generous I am. Come to work for me and I'll throw in whatever it is you shoved down the back of your jeans."

Laverne lifted one side of the ugly plastic cap covering both of her ears. "What'd she say?"

"Nothing!" My ears began to burn. "Laverne? I'll meet you outside. I just want to talk to Geraldine for a minute. About *the job*."

"Oh! Fantastic!" Laverne scurried toward the door. "I'll go crank up the AC in the Lincoln, so it'll be nice and cool for you!"

I forced a smile. "Great. You do that."

Laverne winked and patted me on the shoulder as she passed by. "Break a leg, Honey!" Then she pranced out the door, modeling her plastic babushka as if it were a tiara she'd just won in a senior beauty pageant in Krapstanistan.

I closed the thrift-shop door behind Laverne, then turned off my fake smile and glared at Geraldine. "What makes you think I have something in my jeans?"

The old lady smirked. "I can see the bulge. If it were a tail, I'm pretty sure I'd have seen you on the news."

"Ugh!" I pulled the Hummel from the back of my pants.

"Happy Traveler," Geraldine said, taking it from me.

"Huh?"

"That's the name of the figurine. But I have to say, I'm not so sure this little guy'd leave a five-star review about his trip down your butt crack."

I gritted my teeth. "Hilarious. Look. You got your stupid figurine back. I'm leaving." I turned to go. "Oh, and good luck finding somebody."

"Not so fast," Geraldine said. "Shoplifting anything worth $300 or more is a third-degree felony in Florida. Punishable by prison time, I might add."

"What!" I whirled back around. "Sure, I took that thing from Lulu's—I mean *Laverne's* box. But I did it *before* you said you'd take it off her hands. So technically, it wasn't yours at the time I took it."

Geraldine raised an unkempt silver eyebrow. "And just who's gonna corroborate your story?"

"Laverne, of course!" I glanced out the window. Laverne was in her Continental, still wearing that idiotic polka-dotted cap. She was smiling and chirping at her reflection in the rearview mirror like a demented parakeet.

Geraldine smirked. "Not sure how I see that one playing out in court. How about you?"

A vein on my right temple began to throb. "And if I take the stupid job?"

Geraldine's face broke into a grandmotherly smile. "Then all is well. No cops. No questions. I'll even throw in little mister Happy Traveler, here, as a token of my good faith."

I'd have loved to throw in a fist to her nose as a token of *my* good faith. But a criminal record would've been the last nail in the coffin for me ever finding a decent job one day. I also had Tom to consider. I'd already put him through enough of my shenanigans over the years. Did he really deserve to see me become another embarrassing headline for our state?

Florida Woman Caught with "Happy Traveler" on Tour of Her Nether Regions

I closed my eyes, took a deep breath, and resigned myself to my fate. "Fine. I'll do it. You win."

Geraldine nodded confidently. "I usually do. Okay. Grab a broom and let's get started."

"What? I can't. I'm riding with Laverne. Geez! At least let me go home and get my own car."

"Fine. Never let it be said that I'm not a reasonable person." Geraldine glanced at the faded, gold-tone watch on her wrist. "But if you're not back here in an hour, I'm calling the cops."

Chapter Eleven

On the drive home, I pretended to listen as Laverne prattled on excitedly about my new job. But how could I possibly concentrate? Since getting up this morning, I'd been fired from Tiffany's Temps, fleeced by Marco Shamway, quite likely dumped by my boyfriend, threatened by some random mystery attorney, and now I'd just been blackmailed into working for an old lady in a junk store for peanuts.

My Mercury wasn't in retrograde. It had hit a freaking grenade!

I didn't even dare imagine what else could possibly go wrong before my head hit the pillow tonight. And if Laverne didn't step on it, that pillow was going to be a cot at the county jail. Her old old-lady driving had already eaten up over half of the 60 minutes Geraldine Jiggles had allotted me to get back to her shop before she called the cops and ratted me out for shoplifting.

Come on, Laverne!

I stared out the passenger window, drumming my nails on the door handle and mashing my imaginary gas pedal.

Aliens? If you're up there, now would be a really good time to beam me aboard.

• • • •

WITH 24 MINUTES LEFT on my doomsday clock, Laverne finally pulled the Lincoln Continental up to her house.

"We'll do donuts another time," I said, jumping out of her car before she came to a full stop in her driveway.

"Sure, Honey," she called out as I made a mad dash across her lawn and over to my own front yard.

After tripping over a sprinkler head, I made a stumbling recovery, then scrambled into the driver's seat of my old

Falcon convertible. I jammed the key in the ignition, cranked the engine, and peeled out of my driveway.

T-minus 21 minutes to criminal record...

As I raced past Laverne's house, she smiled and waved at me like I was jolly Saint Nick in the annual Christmas parade.

I shook my head.

Geez. Maybe ignorance really is bliss.

• • • •

EVEN WITH HITTING MOSTLY green lights and flying over the Corey Causeway with all four tires in the air, I made it back to Belated Rooms with only 37 seconds to spare. I used two of those seconds to check my face in the rearview mirror. Not for makeup, but for *attitude.*

I wasn't even working for Geraldine Jiggles yet and she already had me jumping through hoops like Laverne's condo committee. I'd gone from dignified human to trained Chihuahua in 59.5 minutes flat.

Over the years, I'd taken some really crummy jobs for some even crummier reasons. But *blackmail*? This was a new low even for *me.*

Well played, Geraldine Jiggles. Well played.

I blew out a frustrated breath and unhooked my seatbelt. Like a kid headed to the doctor's office for a shot in the keister, I reluctantly hauled myself out of Shabby Maggie, resigned myself to my fate.

As I reached for the front door of Belated Rooms, through the grimy glass I made out a shriveled, bespectacled face smirking at me like the Cheshire Skunk. I gritted my teeth.

Geez. No wonder Jerry didn't show up for work. Slaving away in this junk heap with that crazy old lady? It's gotta be like working on a garbage barge with Voldemort.

I took a deep breath and pushed open the squeaky front door.

"Another ten seconds and I'd have had to dock you," Geraldine said, tapping the watch circling her liver-spotted wrist.

"Yeah?" I grumbled. "It's kinda hard to dock someone's pay when they haven't earned anything yet, isn't it?"

"Not really," the old woman said. "Not if you know the right tricks."

Chapter Twelve

O f all the disgusting things I'd imagined I'd be forced to do working for Geraldine Jiggles, having to take her mandatory course in salesmanship hadn't even crossed my mind. Yet here I was, being schooled by a huckster sporting a number 2 pencil behind her ear and a dead skunk atop her head.

Geraldine pushed her green bifocals up on her nose, then pulled the pencil from behind her ear. She pointed the rubber end of it at a heap of junkyard fodder dumped on top of a cheap folding table.

"Okay, Fremden. Lesson number one. Remember these three letters. V-S-D."

My upper lip snarled. "What's that? Some kind of disease I can catch by touching that stuff?"

"No!" She swatted me on the wrist with the pencil...*hard.* "VSD stands for Valuable. Saleable. Disposable. Those are the three principles on which I run my establishment, smart ass."

I frowned and rubbed the red mark on my wrist. "I noticed *integrity* wasn't one of them."

Geraldine cocked her head and glared at me. "You want I should call the cops or what?"

I adjusted my attitude. "No, ma'am."

The crotchety old woman reached into the pile of junk and plucked out a dirty, half-naked plastic baby doll. "So, what do you think this is? V, S, or D?"

I studied the doll with the odd, spaghetti-like hair molded onto its skull. It was missing an arm, an eye, and appeared to have suffered a fatal gunshot wound to the back.

"Disposable?" I asked. "Kind of looks like it's been murderized to me."

"No!" Geraldine delivered another whack to my wrist with her lethal pencil. "Lesson one, Fremden: *Nothing* is disposable! You know that old saying, one man's trash is another man's treasure?"

"Yes." I rubbed my wrist and took a step out of range.

Geraldine took a step toward me and shook her pencil in my face. "Nothing is trash until it either rots, disintegrates, or shatters into a million pieces. Otherwise, you mine the value. Got it?"

"Um ... *mine the value*?"

"Yes! As in *dig* for it." The old woman shoved the doll into my hand. "Come on. I'll show you."

Holding the nasty, dismembered doll between two pinched fingers, I trailed behind Geraldine as she tromped over to the Plexiglass checkout stand. She dragged a ragged old book from beneath the heaps of papers piled beside the cash register. Then she cracked open the weathered tome and skimmed through its tattered pages.

"Aha!" she said.

My nose crinkled. "What?"

"Check the doll's butt crack."

I blanched. "Excuse me?"

Geraldine glared at me. "You got wax in your ears?"

"No." I gingerly pulled down the yellowed diaper hiding what was left of the mangled doll's dignity.

"What's it say?" Geraldine demanded.

I cringed with disgust. "That you're some kind of pervert?"

"Ugh! Gimme that!" Geraldine snatched the doll from my hands, spread its legs, and studied the place where its genitalia would've been, had the manufacturer been so kind as to provide it with any.

"See this number running along here?" she asked.

I didn't want to look. "Uh ... how about I take your word for it?"

Geraldine shot me some side-eye, then ran a gnarled index finger along a page of the book. "Heh," she grunted, then looked up at me and grinned smugly.

"Just as I suspected. Fremden, you're looking at a genuine 1963 Horseman Baby Doll. *Plastic Wets*. That hole in its back? That's where you pour in the water to make it pee. It's worth 25 bucks, vintage."

"Vintage, as in old?" I asked.

"No. As in undamaged."

"Oh. And what's it worth in its um ... *current* condition?"

Geraldine blew out a sigh and tossed the doll back to me. I caught it, albeit unwillingly.

"Says in the book there's no market for parts," she said, slamming the book closed. "I guess we'll have to sell it for whatever we can get for it."

Yeah. Good luck with that.

• • • •

OVER THE COURSE OF the afternoon, Geraldine took me on an extensive, three-hour tour of the inner workings of Belated Rooms. Like the castaways on *Gilligan's Island*, I spent the entire time trying to figure out how to escape.

But I was doomed. With Geraldine breathing down my neck it was Belated Rooms or the Pinellas County Jail. So, I tagged along and feigned interest as the old lady explained how she'd segmented her dingy little thrift store universe into four separate galaxies.

First stop on the tour was the obsolete kitchen-gadget graveyard stocked with old toasters, microwaves, and blenders that had made their last frozen margaritas sometime before the first Clinton administration.

Second came the grungy "Kiddie Corner" (aka dead toy emporium) piled with dirty, scuffed, hand-me-down toys and an old wooden crib straight out of *Rosemary's Baby*.

The third area in the quadrangle of junk was the used-and-abused furniture department. I was pretty sure some sketchy stuff had gone down on the ugly brown couch in the corner. But it barely compared to the horrors that had been experienced by what I dubbed, "the Mattress of Mysterious Stains."

The fourth corner contained the clothing section. Its rusty racks were crammed with outfits that, like me, would probably wait forever in vain to become fashionable again. The aroma coming off them contributed greatly to Belated Rooms' signature smell.

"So, what do you think?" Geraldine asked.

"I've never seen anything quite like it," I said.

Geraldine beamed with pride over her odd assortment of dumpster filler. I wasn't quite so enthusiastic. Maybe it was just me, but the whole place was kind of creepy—a reminder of the kind of life nobody wanted to live anymore. By the time the tour was over, I felt the twinge of clinical depression setting in.

"So, that just leaves the contract," Geraldine said as she headed back toward the cash register.

I blanched. "Contract? I thought I was just helping you out temporarily."

"You are. But I can't leave you in charge of all of this without some kind of legal protection now, can I?"

"Are you kidding?" I stuck a thumb to my chest. "*I'm* the one who needs protection. After all, *you're* the one who blackmailed *me* into this."

Geraldine smiled coyly. "Come come, Fremden. Blackmail is such an ugly word. Cheer up. If you want, I can add a clause at the end that says if you fulfill your employment obligations and return my shop to me in one piece, I'll owe you $150. I'll even throw in an excellent reference. How's that sound?"

Like ransom added to blackmail, that's what.

I gritted my teeth. "A hundred and fifty bucks for four days worth of work?"

"Maybe just three, depending on my luck at the slots." Geraldine wagged a boney finger in my face. "And don't forget. You also get that Hummel. And no police record."

I frowned. "Fine. But I want that second part in writing, too. And on a separate piece of paper from the contract."

Geraldine grinned as if she'd already hit the slots jackpot. "Deal."

• • • •

I WAS DEBATING WHETHER to just chuck it all and make a run for it when the thrift shop's front door creaked open. An older man with an unfortunate bulbous nose and an even more unfortunate scraggly ponytail walked in.

He spotted me, then looked at Geraldine and said, "Oh. I didn't know you had a customer."

"Nah," Geraldine said. "This is just my new employee, Val Fremden."

I waved like a hostage with a gun to my back. "Hi."

"Nice to meet you, Val. I'm Davy Eber. I run the antiques shop two doors down. Eber Antiques."

"Oh." I offered him a half-hearted smile. "Nice to meet you."

"Yeah, yeah. Enough with the niceties," Geraldine said. "Hey Davy, I gotta show you the load I got off a ditzy old broad this morning. Hummels! A whole horde of them!"

Davy's stoner eyes took on a sudden gleam. "Really?"

"Yes, really," I grumbled.

Davy shot me a cautious glance. "Yours?"

I frowned. "No. Somebody I know."

Geraldine slapped Davy on the back. "Come take a look. I got these gems all lined up on the shelves in the storeroom. Just waiting for you to take your pick."

"Sweet," Davy said, then smiled and showed us his unfortunate teeth.

Ugh. Maybe he'll spend some of the profits from the Hummels on some decent dental work.

As Davy turned to go with Geraldine, I took a step to follow them. Geraldine shot me a look. "Where do you think you're going, Fremden? Stay here and mind the register."

"Why?" I asked. "You haven't had a single customer all afternoon."

"Yes, I have." Geraldine smiled smugly. "You're looking right at him."

I frowned and glumly watched as the pair headed toward a gray door at the back of the store. Geraldine unlocked it. Davy opened the door, took a step inside, and blurted, "Holy Hummel Heaven!"

As angry as I was about poor J.D.'s fortune in Hummels getting sold out from under him, I was powerless to do anything about it. I couldn't very well rat out Laverne now, could I?

About a quarter hour later, after much clinking and rustling in the back room, I heard Geraldine say, "Well, that about wraps that up, Davy. Good doing business with you."

I looked up from the register to see her and Davy emerging from the back storage room. Geraldine locked the door behind her, then followed Davy up to the front door. In his tattooed arms he toted a box that appeared packed to the gills. On the side of the carton, I recognized the handwritten initials on it.

I cringed. J.D. was being fleeced using his own moving boxes.

"Let Fremden get the door for you," Geraldine said, shooting me a *make yourself useful* look.

I shuffled over and opened the door. Davy thanked me, then disappeared down the sidewalk, whistling as he made off with J.D.'s precious cargo.

I closed the door and glared at Geraldine. "You're all smiles and giggles."

She laughed and counted out a fistful of paper money. "You would be too if you'd just made an easy two grand and had plane tickets to Vegas in the morning."

As much as I desperately wanted to, I simply couldn't argue with that.

Chapter Thirteen

Not a single other customer darkened the doors of Belated Rooms the rest of the afternoon. At 5 p.m. sharp, Geraldine locked the place up and set me free for the evening—with a warning not to violate the terms of my parole.

"I better see you back here at 8 a.m. sharp, or else!" she said, then hobbled over to an old red pickup truck that appeared to have almost survived a firebombing at some point.

I watched Geraldine's rusty old truck disappear down Corey Avenue, then headed for Shabby Maggie. As I reached for the car door, I spotted a thin black woman across the street, near the movie theater. She was hauling something in a wheelbarrow. She stopped and waved at me.

"Hey!" she called out across the road. "Is the junk store still open?"

I shook my head. "Nope. Just closed."

"Darn. You wanna buy this stuff?"

"I dunno," I called back. "What've you got?"

"Some first-class bric-a-brac!" She bent over, reached into the wheelbarrow, and pulled out a figurine.

Kaching!

"Hold on!" I crossed the road, digging through the bottom of my purse for loose change. "How much for the figurine?"

She held it up. It was a cheesy bodybuilder in a speedo, striking a pose.

It reminded me of Marco. I had to have it.

"Two bucks and it's yours," she said.

"What? It's got a big chip on its shoulder."

"Fine. Make me an offer."

I held out my open palm, displaying the cache scrounged from the bottom of my purse. "Will you take this?"

The woman eyed the dime, two nickels, three pennies, half a roll of breath mints, and an unused postage stamp. Her brow furrowed with a tinge of *what the hell?*

"You really that desperate for this thing?" she asked.

I nodded. "You have no idea."

"Okay, then, Honey. It's yours."

"Thank you!" I gushed and grabbed the figurine from her hand. "You're a lifesaver!"

"Huh. Nobody ever called me that before. What's your name?"

"Val."

She held out a hand to shake. "Needra. I hope you and your little friend there will be very happy."

"We will," I said, already anticipating the rush of smashing Marco's effigy to dust. "I promise."

I headed back to my car with a spring in my step. I waved to Needra, shifted into reverse, and peeled out, endorphins buzzing my brain.

Marco Shamway, prepare to die!

Maggie's tires squealed. I laughed maniacally. Then I caught a glimpse of myself in the rearview mirror.

Geez, Val. Maybe you do *have a smashing problem ...*

• • • •

I WAS HALFWAY HOME when the Falcon's engine began to sputter. The fuel gauge read "E." I was running on fumes.

Reluctantly, I took a left and headed for a gas station. The detour forced me to drive by that blasted billboard of Marco Shamway again. The smug look on his irritatingly handsome face sent my blood boiling once more.

Big, lousy jerk! Why couldn't he at least have had the decency to age badly?

Suddenly, the fingers on my right hand began to twitch. I knew the telltale warning sign all too well. I needed another fix—the kind that only my Hammer of Justice could deliver.

I peeled into the station and reached for my savings passbook. Okay, it was a roll of quarters. I kept it under the driver's seat for emergencies, such as paying parking meters before the meter maid busted me, and turning my purse into an impromptu hacky sack to swing at suspicious creeps.

After forking over the roll to the gas station attendant, it was official. I was flat broke.

• • • •

WHEN I PULLED UP TO my house, I was still jonesing for a little hammer action. I guess that was why I was both mad and glad not to see my boyfriend's silver SUV in the driveway.

On the one hand, with Tom away, I was free to wield my Hammer of Justice with impunity. On the other hand, Tom was apparently still on "special assignment." So, he was either working undercover with his police unit, or he was working under the covers with that floozy on the voicemail message.

I frowned. Tom would have to come clean soon. But then again, so would I. How was I going to explain to him about losing my job, being duped out of a fortune, being caught shoplifting, and sinking to a new low by working in that indoor junkyard, Belated Rooms? Not to mention the whole mystery attorney thing. What was up with that?

I chewed my bottom lip and contemplated driving to Mexico and starting a new life. But then I remembered I didn't have enough pesos to even get out of Pinellas County.

I cut the ignition and pulled out the keys. Maybe staying incommunicado with Tom for the moment was a good thing. Hopefully, with a little luck, I could avoid jail time and find a real job without him even knowing anything about this whole mess. And with a little bit *more* luck, Tom's brain-damage-induced attraction to me would last until we both kicked the bucket.

Chapter Fourteen

F or some reason, last night I couldn't find my Hammer of Justice. I thought I'd left it in the garage after my last porcelain pounding episode. Nonetheless, I'd improvised and used Tom's instead. Of course, it wasn't quite the same. But I'm a Southern gal, so I was used to making do.

After pounding back two of Tom's beers and putting the hammer down on that weightlifter figurine, I'd fallen asleep on the couch and slept like a baby. But as I pulled Shabby Maggie up to Belated Rooms at 7:59 this morning, I wondered if I was still just a tad tipsy.

The entire front of the thrift shop appeared to be moving in and out of focus—as if it were dematerializing into some kind of weird, interstellar portal.

That's what I get for falling asleep to Dr. Who *reruns.*

I blinked twice, but the bizarre view didn't change. I grabbed my cheater glasses from atop the dashboard and took a closer look. That's when I realized the entire storefront was crawling with ugly beige bugs the size of my thumb. I shook my head and grimaced in disgust.

Okay, Val. This has got to be a sign from God. Working at Belated Rooms is a bad idea of Biblical proportions.

"Screw it," I muttered. "I'm outta here."

I shifted into reverse and began backing out of the parking spot. Before I'd gone two feet, Geraldine came racing out the front door of her intergalactic demon-possessed thrift shop.

"Where you going?" she screeched, her skunk hair flapping in the hot morning breeze.

"Haven't you noticed?" I nodded toward the creepy crawlies swarming all over the shop windows. "What happened? You forget to exorcize the place before you left last night?"

"Ugh! Don't be a baby," Geraldine said. "It's just a few mole crickets, for crying out loud. Get in here, Fremden! I've only got an hour to finish showing you the ropes. My plane leaves at one!"

For a moment my foot hovered between the brake and the accelerator ... between work and freedom ... between life and death. I was a millisecond from flooring the gas when an image of Tom's face flashed in my mind. Then an image of me locked in a jail cell.

The air went out of me like a punctured tire. I shifted gears and eased Maggie back into the parking spot.

• • • •

"AND THAT'S HOW YOU run the register. Got it?" Geraldine asked.

"Yeah."

"And don't think you can skim money from the till without me knowing."

I frowned. "But you said all this crap ... *merchandise* ... is negotiable. How would you know if I was being straight with you or not?"

Geraldine's eyes narrowed and locked onto mine. "I have my ways."

My brow furrowed. "*What* ways?"

"Never you mind."

"Fine." I let out a long breath and glanced around Belated Rooms' storehouse of junk. "How do I price stuff that comes in?"

Geraldine's lips puckered. "I'd tell you to use your best judgment, but I think that ship has sailed."

Considering I'd just signed on for a long weekend cruise aboard a bug-infested, junk-filled garbage trawler, I had to concede her point.

"Listen, Fremden. If they don't offer the stuff for free, before you buy anything, look it up in those books I showed you. Find the retail price and offer them a third for it."

"And if the stuff isn't in the books?"

She shrugged. "Anything you can get for under two bucks, just do it. If you're not sure, ask Davy. He's a walking encyclopedia of antiques."

Yeah. So is his hairstyle and clothes.

The front door creaked. Geraldine's attention shifted toward it. "Speak of the devil. You come for the rest of the haul?"

"Yeah," Davy said. Then he smiled at me, making me wish he hadn't.

"Right this way," Geraldine said, her lips a smarmy carnival barker smile. The pair headed for the storage room. When they returned a few minutes later, Davy was toting another of J.D.'s boxes.

"Good doing business with you, Jiggles," he said as she opened the door for him. "Good luck in Vegas."

She laughed. "Thanks for the gamblin' money. Take a good look at this face, Davy. If I hit it big, you won't be seeing me around here no more."

"What are the odds of that?" Davy asked.

"Eh, a girl can dream, can't she?" Geraldine said.

A roach crawled across the countertop in front of me.

Yep. That's some kind of dream you got here, Jiggles.

As Davy disappeared out the door, so did Geraldine's kitschy saleswoman charm. "Okay, Fremden," she said like a drill sergeant. "I'm outta here. You got any final questions?"

Yeah. What's wrong with my life?

I shrugged. "I guess not."

"Alrighty then." Geraldine handed me the keys and headed for the door. "Oh. And if Jerry shows up looking for his last paycheck, tell him to stuff it. If he gives you any grief, call the cops. I've got them on speed dial on the landline. Just press lucky number seven."

My nose crinkled. "You've got the cops on speed dial?"

Geraldine winked. "A woman can never be too careful now, can she?"

I grimaced. "I guess not."

As Geraldine headed for the door, I glanced around the shelves beneath the cash register. "Oh!" I called out. "I've got a question!"

The old lady whirled around, her face the poster child for annoyance. "What? Make it quick!"

"Uh ... where do you keep the bug spray?"

"In the storeroom. But take my advice. Don't use it on the bums hanging around here. For some reason, the cops consider that 'assault.'"

"Bums? What am I supposed—"

But it was too late. Geraldine was already out the door.

Chapter Fifteen

They say there's a fine line between trash and treasure. If that's true, Geraldine Jiggles stumbled over that line like a drunk failing a roadside sobriety test.

A cracked crockpot? A ceiling fan with one blade? A chair with no seat bottom? Who in their right mind would buy any of this crap?

I glanced around at the piles of useless crap filling the thrift shop. Suddenly, I felt the walls begin to close in on me.

What if a tornado blew through this place and I got caught up in a swirling mass with all this junk? How long would it take rescuers to find my body? What if I died in here?

Geez. Don't be so dramatic, Val. You're not gonna die in here.

Then I spotted something that changed my mind. It was that horrible, one-eyed baby doll, Plastic Wets. The poor, cycloptic lump of plastic was staring at me from its lopsided perch atop the Plexiglass countertop.

What if that thing is cursed! What if it's the grandpa of Chucky in Child's Play*? I could be its next victim!*

I shot it a horrified glare. "What are *you* looking at?"

Thank God, it didn't answer. But I was still totally weirded out by it. I marched over and grabbed Chucky Junior by the noggin and twirled its dirty, one-eyed head around so it faced the front door.

"There. Keep an eye out for *customers*, not *me*."

Keep an eye out?

My unintentional pun made me laugh. But then a weird shiver ran up my spine.

Geez. Is this how the doll's curse begins? Me laughing at it?

An eerie squeal sounded to my right. I gasped and whirled around, fully expecting to be mauled by Plastic Wets' cousin emerging from its lair somewhere amidst the Kiddie Corner.

But it had only been the toad squeak of the front door opening. My gut flopped with relief as I watched a plump, harried-looking woman with a headful of frizzy red hair come barging in.

"Where is he?" she demanded.

"Chucky?" I asked.

"No. Jerry. He's supposed to be working today."

"Oh. Um ... I took his place."

"Jerk!"

My right eyebrow crooked upward. "Excuse me?"

"Not you." Her tone softened. "I meant Jerry. The bum owes me three months child support."

"Oh."

I studied the woman. The look on her face made me think that if she ever found Jerry, he might not survive the encounter. Not that I'd blame her.

"Sorry," I said. "But Jerry didn't show up for work yesterday, so Geraldine hired me as his replacement."

"Crap." The woman began digging through her huge handbag. "Do me a favor? If you see him, have him call me?"

"Sure."

"Wait. Scratch that." The woman pulled a wallet from her purse and handed me a business card. "If you see him, call *me* instead. This guy's as slippery as a greased eel."

"I would, Lily," I said, reading her name off the card, "but I don't know what Jerry looks like."

"Oh." Lily flashed me a picture in her wallet. It was a family trio. Her, a baby, and a surprisingly handsome looking charmer. "Skipped out on us without a word," she said between clenched teeth.

77

I shook my head. "What a dirtbag. I'll keep an eye out for him. I promise."

"Thanks." Lily's shoulders slumped, as if she'd used up her supply of bravado.

"I hope you find him," I said.

"Yeah. Thanks." She smiled blankly, then turned and left.

I watched her go, then turned back toward the yellowed Plexiglass cashier counter. That hideous one-eyed, one-armed doll was staring back at me again with its one remaining creepy peeper.

"Geez!" I hissed. "Stop doing that!"

• • • •

THE REST OF THE MORNING dragged by like a one-legged centipede. Bored and drowsy, I figured I might as well take a nap. But there was one thing I needed to do first. I stuffed that one-eyed doll in a paper sack and stapled it shut.

I figured if the bag didn't hold Plastic Wets at bay, at least the paper would crinkle and alert me if it tried to make a murderous crawl toward me. Satisfied, I lay down on a plaid couch that smelled like cigarettes and dog butts.

I'd just nodded off when the shop door squeaked open again. I jumped up and wiped the drool from the corner of my mouth. A man was standing a few feet inside the door, blinking weirdly and looking bewildered.

"Can I help you?" I called across the shop to him.

The guy was a standard-issue Florida man. Red-faced Caucasian. Sweaty. Bald. Beer belly. Ugly sandals. Hawaiian shirt. Baggy cargo shorts. Unkempt beard. The only thing he was missing was the cigar.

"Yeah," he called back. "You got any dolls?"

My automatic deviant detector activated. "Dolls? Uh ... any particular kind?"

"Yeah. One with a removable head."

His comment set my perv radar pinging like a full-on invasion. But then I remembered Geraldine's last words to me, "The sale must go on."

"Uh, yes, I think so," I said.

Sensing a chance to kill two birds with one stone, I walked over to the Plexiglass counter and grabbed the paper sack. I ripped it open and pulled out the one-eyed doll. "How about this one? It's a beauty. Just got it in yesterday."

The guy frowned. "It's only got one eye."

I shrugged. "Does it need two eyes for your um ... *intended usage?*"

The guy's brow furrowed into sweaty creases. "I guess not. But its head doesn't come off."

I shoved the doll at him. "Nothing a little hacksaw action couldn't solve."

The guy's mouth twisted as he turned the doll over in his hands and examined its backside.

Gross.

I snuck a surreptitious glance at the landline phone. If the creep pulled the doll's diaper down, I was gonna call the cops. No wonder Geraldine had them on speed dial.

"How much?" he asked.

"Five bucks."

He sneered at me. "For a doll with no eye and no arm?"

"Exactly. That's what makes it one of a kind."

The guy locked his beady eyes with mine. "You take a check?"

"Not on your life."

He smirked. "You at least got a bag I can put it in?"

"Sure." Having just torn up the only paper bag handy, I grabbed a used plastic grocery bag from the heap on the counter. "I'll even throw in the sack for free."

The guy snorted and peeled a sweaty fiver from his back pocket. "You're a real princess."

And you're a real pervert.

"Just go ahead and lay the money on the counter," I said, not wanting to touch the bill.

"As you wish, Princess." He spread the limp five-note out on the counter like a damp loincloth.

I shook my head.

If poor old Lincoln only knew where his face would end up.

I stuffed the one-eyed doll into the grocery bag and handed it over the counter to the guy.

"Nice doing business with you," he said.

I didn't return the sentiment. Instead, I simply watched the guy walk out the door.

Ka-ching!

I'd just made my first sale. Now all I needed was a can of Lysol, a hot shower, and a blow-dryer.

Chapter Sixteen

W hile I waited for Abe Lincoln to dry out, I swept up the dead mole crickets that had made it through the thrift shop's door, but not past my can of Raid. I was dumping a dustpan full of the disgusting creatures into the wastebasket by the cash register when the front door squeaked open again.

I looked up to see the familiar face of a longtime friend. We'd first met in gym class in seventh grade. "Milly! What are *you* doing here?"

The gorgeous blonde grinned. "Just dropped by to check out your new work digs." She glanced around and sniffed. Her face puckered. "Geez, Val. Who died in here?"

I grimaced. "I forgot about the smell. I guess I've gone nose blind. I think it's coming mostly from the clothes. And maybe the sofas."

Milly stared at a jumbled rack crammed with rumpled shirts and dresses. "Wow. I haven't seen clothing this out-of-date since the Renaissance Fair."

I smirked. "Not everybody's a fashionista like you. How have you been?"

"Okay, I guess."

But Milly didn't look okay. The persnickety, upper-crust beauty appeared horrified—as if continued exposure to the detritus of common man might cause her to catch some deadly, agonizing disease. Like povertyitis, or something.

It couldn't. Could it?

"Do you have time for lunch?" she asked, edging toward the front door.

"Sure. Why not." I hadn't had a customer since doll-head guy. "Nothing much going on here."

Milly beamed. "Great!"

I bent down to grab my purse from under the counter. "But we need to stay nearby. I have to keep an eye on the place. I hear the café on the corner is pretty good."

I stood up and looked around the shop. "Milly?" I called out. But she wasn't there. She'd already fled the store, and was waving at me through the window.

• • • •

IT WAS BARELY 11:30. Being so early, Milly and I were the first customers to enter the Friendly Fish Café. I could tell the fish on the sign was friendly because it was grinning at us as if it couldn't wait to jump into a deep fryer and become our own personal sandwich filet.

"Take whatever seat you want," the waitress said, handing us a couple of sticky, laminated menus. "I'll be back in a minute."

Milly and I scooted into a booth upholstered in ripped red vinyl. I situated myself clear of a lump of yellowed foam rubber peeking out from a rupture.

"What do you recommend?" I asked the waitress when she came back toting an order pad.

"A better dishwasher," Milly said. She crinkled her nose. "My fork still has egg yolk on it."

"The shrimp salad sandwich," the waitress said, ignoring Milly. She pointed to a chalkboard on the wall above our heads. "It's today's special."

I nodded. "Sounds good. I'll take it. And a ginger ale, please."

"Make it two," Milly said. "But an iced tea for me. Unsweetened. With two fresh lemon wedges."

The waitress looked Milly up and down and raised an envious eyebrow. "You want those wedges cut straight or on a diagonal?"

"Oh, I'll leave that to you," Milly said without a hint of snark.

Blonde, blue-eyed, and sporting a perfect button nose, Milly had the kind of face that made men swoon and women grind their teeth to dust. If she hadn't also happened to have a heart of gold to match her looks, I probably wouldn't have had any molars left to chew my shrimp salad sandwich.

The waitress returned and plunked our drinks down onto the table. As she left, Milly grabbed my hand and stared at me with concerned, puppy-dog eyes. "Oh, Val. I'm so sorry to see you in such a state."

"Crap." I looked down at my shirt. "Did I spill something on myself already?"

"No. I'm talking about working at that awful place. Blown-Up Rooms."

"*Belated* Rooms." I shrugged. "It's not the worst job I've ever had."

Milly grimaced. "Then what on earth *was*?"

I sighed. "Okay. I'll admit this thrift store gig isn't exactly my dream job."

Milly nodded. "I would hope not. You need to go for your dream job, and not settle for less!"

"If I knew what that was, then maybe I could find it." I frowned and grabbed my ginger ale. "Maybe I'm just not the kind of person who gets the shining light."

"The shining light?"

"Like Laverne. With her shining Lady of the Wiener Cart."

Milly's perfect brow grew a crease. "Her lady of the *what*?"

I shook my head. "Never mind. Long story. How are things with you?"

A light switched on in Milly's sympathetic blue eyes. "Vance and I are doing great! And guess what? Mr. Maas finally retired. I'm heading up the accounting firm now!"

"That's awesome!" I gushed. It was a lie, but well intended. To me, sitting in a cubicle all day doing math and shuffling papers was a fate worse than ... well, almost anything except working at Belated Rooms.

"Aww, thanks," Milly said. Suddenly, her bright face crumpled. "But I hate it that all my dreams came true, and you ended up with the worst job in the world."

I shrugged. "It isn't so bad. I've already gotten to sweep up heaps of bugs, and got to watch a freak show for free."

"Huh?"

I leaned in over the table. "You won't believe this, but my first and only customer this morning was a guy looking for a doll with a removable head."

Milly gasped.

I laughed. "Given all the crap that's landed on my head in the last 24 hours, that pervert is the least of my worries."

"What kind of crap are you talking about?"

I shook my head. "Milly, let me just say that yesterday was the kind of day that inspired the term 'day drinking.'"

Milly's eyes turned to pools of liquid concern. "Oh, no. Val. Don't tell me you've gone and gotten yourself in another one of your tangled-up messes."

I grimaced. "Okay. I won't tell you."

Milly sat up and straightened her shoulders. "Yes, you will, Val Fremden! And right now. Whatever it is, I can help. You're my best friend, for Pete's sake!"

I blew out a sigh. "Fine. Remember Marco Shamway? That jerk from high school?"

"The one who ran your underpants up the flagpole?"

I closed my eyes and pinched the bridge of my nose. "For the millionth time, they were my *mom's* underwear. I'd borrowed them because ... Ugh! Never mind. Anyway, yes. *That* Marco Shamway."

"What about him?"

"He's back in town."

"So?"

I fished my cell phone from my purse, flipped to the picture of Marco on the billboard, and handed it to Milly.

She raised a blonde eyebrow. "Gee. He's hardly changed a bit!"

"I know. Disgusting, isn't it? Anyway, did you happen to notice his ... um ... crotch area?"

Milly squinted at the screen. "Wait. What is that? A clock?"

"Not just any clock. A *Hunk Clock.*"

Milly's eyes grew wide. "But Val, that was *your* idea!"

"I know! But I never had the money to do anything about it. Marco stole my plan, and now he's a freaking millionaire!"

Milly stared at me, mouth agape. Finally, she said, "Life is so unfair. What can I do to help?"

I blew out a breath. "I dunno. Hold him down while I beat him to death?"

"Val, what you need to do is get that jerk to pay you for your idea!"

I slumped back into the booth. "How? I don't have anything in writing to claim the Hunk Clock was mine."

"Yes, you do. I saw it in your Possibilities Book back in high school. Have you still got it?"

I shot Milly a look. "Has my cousin Tammy still got her virginity? Milly, I threw that thing out years ago, when I realized I had no possibilities."

Milly frowned and took my hand. "Stop beating yourself up, Val. You've got *lots* of possibilities left."

"Yeah? Name one."

Milly winced. "Well, you and Tom might get married, right? He's asked you."

"Yeah. But that's more like a miracle than a possibility. You know what a commitment phobe I am."

Milly frowned and crossed her arms. "That's your whole problem, Val. You don't stick to things. I say this is your moment to start. Get Marco to confess the idea was yours. I'll go with you as your witness. Wait. Better yet, I'll secretly record his confession on my phone!"

"Like he's really going to do that, Milly. Besides, I have no idea how to even get ahold of him."

Milly shot me a coy smile. "Knowing Marco, I bet he's booked himself into a suite at the Don Cesar. That's where all the hotshots stay."

I frowned. "Maybe. But what if we find him and he won't talk to us? Then what?"

Milly chewed a pouty lip. "Maybe we can slash his tires."

"That wouldn't put a dent in what that dirtbag owes me."

"Then sue the rat!"

I scowled. "I'd rather kill him."

"Here you go. Two shrimp salad sandwiches," the waitress said, shooting me an odd look. "You lucky gals got the last two."

I glanced up at her. "I thought you said this was the daily special. We're the only two customers in here."

"Eh," the waitress shrugged and set the plates in front of us. "It's the daily special until it sells out. Eat up. I'm telling you, the customers were *raving* about it yesterday."

Chapter Seventeen

Defying all expectations, the shrimp salad sandwiches at the Friendly Fish were delicious. Milly and I wolfed ours down. In between mouthfuls, we dreamed up creative ways to obliterate Marco Shamway's despicable presence from the face of the Earth.

More than I cared to admit, my schemes mainly involved the forcible insertion of the Hunk Clock into various orifices on Marco's body. Milly's ideas weren't quite so graphic. However, we both agreed on one thing: no matter what kind of crazy scenario we came up with, we first had to find the dirtbag.

Given Marco's arrogant snobbery back in high school, Milly was certain he'd be staying at the fanciest beach hotel around. Namely the elegant and historic Don Cesar. She proposed that we go there to check it out right after lunch. Seeing as how Milly's plan would have me at a luxury resort on the beach instead of trapped in that dingy junk-shop dungeon, it wasn't exactly hard to persuade me.

Twenty minutes later, Milly's shiny red BMW made a right off Gulf Boulevard and into the parking lot beside the huge, pink castle of a hotel. The Don Cesar was situated right on the sugar-white sands of St. Pete Beach. When she rolled down the window to pay for parking, I could smell the salt air.

"Geez. The parking is crazy expensive!" I said as I read the fee sign posted on the lot attendant's booth. "We should've just called the front desk and asked if Marco Shamway was staying here."

"Forget it, Val." Milly said. "This is a fancy hotel. They'd never divulge their guests' names." She reached a manicured hand through the driver's side window and handed the lot attendant a credit card.

The young man in the crisp white uniform glanced down at her card, then shot her a brilliant smile. "And how long will you be staying with us, Ms. Halbert?"

"Just a few hours. We're visiting a friend."

"Very good," he said, and turned to run her card.

I nudged Milly. "How in the world are we gonna find Marco, assuming he's even staying here?"

"That shouldn't be a problem," the lot attendant said. "Ask for Tony. He'll tell you ... if the price is right. Be sure and tell him Donny sent you."

"Thank you, Donny," Milly said. "Put another five on my bill for yourself."

Donny raised an eyebrow. "Gee, thanks."

I thought five bucks had been a generous gesture on Milly's part. But the expression on Donny's face didn't exactly convey that he was impressed—or even grateful. Without another word, he handed Milly back her credit card and parking pass, then opened the gate and let us into the lot.

• • • •

ON OUR WAY TO THE LOBBY, Milly and I walked past the beach bar. I spotted at least a dozen guys lounging by the pool. From a distance and without my cheater glasses, any one of them could've been Marco Shamway. I felt my blood pressure begin to rise.

What would I do if I saw him?

Several slim, attractive young men in crisp khaki shorts and white polo shirts were busy attending the pool guests like worker bees around their queen. I suddenly became aware this probably wasn't exactly the greatest place for a low-rent showdown over money.

"How are we ever gonna find this Tony guy in this crowd?" I asked.

"You let me worry about that," Milly said. "Follow my lead."

Fortunately, as it turned out, neither one of us needed to be Sherlock. As we entered the lobby, the clerk at the front desk was wearing a shiny brass nametag with the name THONII etched on it.

"Geez," I whispered to Milly. "Why do people think spelling their names all weird like that makes them special somehow?"

"Shh!" Milly hissed. "We need this guy on our side. Stay here. I'll go up and ask him about Marco."

I hung back a few feet. Milly sashayed up to the counter and batted her eyelashes at Thonii. It was a signature move I'd seen her perform since junior high. But at age 50, the power of Milly's magic lashes seemed to have faded a notch. Instead of Thonii's eyes boring into Milly with lust, they merely appeared bored.

"What can I do for you, ma'am?" Thonii asked.

The "M" word. Ouch!

"I'm looking for an old school friend of mine," Milly said. "Marco Shamway. He told me to stop by while he was staying here."

Thonii's narrow, snooty face pinched. "I'm sorry, ma'am. I'm not allowed to divulge the names of guests."

I marched up to the desk and slid a scroungy five-dollar bill at the clerk. "Could you tell my buddy Lincoln?"

Thonni lifted his nose another inch. "I'm afraid not."

I frowned. "How about Hamilton?"

"Certainly not," Thonni huffed. "But I'd tell Grant what he wanted to know."

"Hugh Grant?" Milly asked.

"No." I scowled. "He means a fifty. That's too much. Let's get out of here."

We turned to leave. Thonii called out after us. "Wait. I'd tell Grant the guy's room number, too."

• • • •

MILLY AND I DECIDED to save the fifty bucks and have a look around the place first. Thanks to Thonii, we already knew that Marco Shamway was staying here. And on a gorgeous day like today, the guy was most likely at the poolside bar.

We headed to the ladies' room to change into the pair of emergency bathing suits Milly had stuffed into her huge purse. (It's a Florida thing.) Donning her cute, beachy sandals and big sunglasses, Milly looked like a movie star. Donning my wobbly thighs, flip flops, and frizzed-out hair, I looked like her second-string dog-walker.

Milly had already shelled out a bundle just to park. For all that dough, we figured if we couldn't find Marco, we could at least take a dip in the gorgeous pool while we were here. Besides, if we actually *did* spot the jerk, I was definitely going to need to cool off. Big time.

• • • •

MARCO WASN'T AT THE pool. And he wasn't hanging around at the poolside tiki bar. Even though our search was a bust, Milly decided to make the most of it. She ordered us a couple of really expensive fruity cocktails. When they arrived sporting little umbrellas, we decided to wander off in search of our own spot in the shade.

"That dirtbag," I grumbled, lying back on the lounge chair next to Milly. "Where could Marco be?"

"I don't know."

Milly positioned her lovely legs in an elegant, Grace Kelly repose. I was just doing my best not to look like a frog caught in an ace bandage.

"Val, maybe we should go back and pay Thonii the fifty for Marco's room number."

"No. You've already spent more money than I can afford to repay." I poked the straw around in my drink. "Did I tell you that some strange attorney left his card on my door? I wonder if Marco's trying to sue me."

Milly lowered her sunglasses and studied me. "Sue *you*? For what?"

"I dunno. But if it isn't Marco, then who?"

Milly's nose crinkled. "Val? Have you gotten into a scrape I don't know about?"

I squinted up at the sky. "Uh ... not that I can think of."

As if on cue, a small green parrot flew overhead, squawking as it passed. I pictured the staff at Sunken Gardens—then the pizza-pan knot on Melvin Flemster's forehead.

Geez. If I made a new Possibilities Book, it'd be full of iron bars and orange jumpsuits.

"Well, if you ask me, *you* should be the one suing *Marco*," Milly said. "The guy stole your idea, made a fortune with it, and didn't even offer you a dime!"

I took a long sip of my cocktail. "Don't remind me. I already want to kill the dirtbag."

"This Marco dude sounds like a real douche," the man in the lounger beside me said. "Does he happen to be tall, good-looking, and fit as a fiddle?"

I scowled sourly at the guy. "Yeah. Why?"

"I think he sat next to me at the pool yesterday." The man sat up in his lounger, sending a hairy cushion of fat cascading over the top of his bathing suit. "The jerk ripped *me* off, too."

My eyebrows raised an inch. "Seriously? How?"

"He came up to me all friendly like and told me his name was Marco," the man said, then raised an arm and scratched the edge of his mostly receded hairline.

"So, what happened?" I asked, trying not to grimace. The guy had more hair on his back than on his entire head.

"This Marco guy took the lounge chair beside me and started ordering shots of Patron for me and him." He laughed and shook his head. "Stupid me. I thought I'd hit the jackpot. We finished off the bottle, then he says he's gotta take a leak. The scumbag left and never came back. Stuck me with the tab. Over $300."

I gritted my teeth. "What a jerk!"

"Yeah. You ain't kiddin'." The guy shrugged, causing his man-boobs to jiggle. "Good thing I'm loaded, eh? Do me a favor. If you find this jerk, kill him again for me, too, would you?"

"And a third time for me," a woman's voice sounded to my left. I turned to see a waitress holding a tray. Her name tag read Jeri. She was clad in the same white polo shirt and beige khakis as the men, only her shorts were a good ten inches higher up her thighs.

"What'd Marco do to you?" Milly asked.

"He stood me up last night, that's what!" Jeri said. "Didn't even have the decency to call and let me know he couldn't make it."

I scowled. "Jeri, did you get his phone number?"

She frowned. "No. But the jerk's got mine. I hope he calls just so I can hang up on him and block his sorry ass."

"Uh ... Jeri?" Milly asked. "You wouldn't happen to know what room he's in, perchance?"

Jeri shook her head, then looked to her left, then right. "I'm sorry, Miss. I can't tell you that. But I *can* recommend today's special. It's *number 22*."

"Thanks," Milly said. "But we've already had lunch."

The waitress shot me a look. "I got it," I said. "Milly, we should pay the lady and get out of here."

"No need," Jeri said. "Your drinks are on the house. The only payment I need is for you to kick Marco for me when you find him. Make sure it's where the sun don't shine."

"You got it," I said. "And thanks for the drinks. With the prices around here, we owe you at least one swift one to his family jewels."

"Ouch," said the fat guy beside me. "You gals are vicious!"

Jeri laughed. "We gotta stick together, right?" She winked at Milly and me, then turned and left to tend to another guy a few chairs away.

I turned to Milly. "Well, we got what we came for. Let's get out of here before we turn into lobsters like the rest of these folks."

"Why waste your time chasing that loser Marco?" the guy in the lounger asked as we got up to leave. "Not when you've got a winner like me ready to take you two pretty ladies out on the town."

"Sorry. We're both taken," I said. "She's married, and I'm ... uh ... working on it."

At least as far as I know ...

"That's a crying shame." The guy flopped back onto his lounger like a hairy harbor seal. "Well, if you change your mind, I'm in room 39. Name's Don McLester. What's yours?"

I stifled a groan. "Uh ...

I'm Thelma. And this is my friend Louise."

Chapter Eighteen

Even knowing Marco Shamway's room number at the Don Cesar, our mission to track him down ultimately turned out to be a bust. Milly and I'd knocked on his door at least five times, but no one ever answered. When a housekeeper gave us the stank eye and reached for her walkie-talkie, we'd decided to beat a hasty retreat and try again tomorrow.

"Pick you up at eleven?" Milly asked as she dropped me off at Belated Rooms.

"Sounds good." I waved goodbye to Milly and her red Beemer and dragged myself back inside the junk shop. I glanced at the clock on the wall and groaned. It was only 2 p.m. Three more hours of this place was going to be an eternity.

My first order of business was to return the grungy five-dollar bill I'd "borrowed" from the till in case of emergency. Thankfully, I hadn't had to spend it on bribing Thonii, so technically I hadn't sunk to thievery. I still had some principles left—unlike that lowlife scumbag Marco Shamway.

A pinch of Southern pride shot through me. I straightened my shoulders and pulled myself together. Was Belated Rooms where I wanted to be at this point in my life? No. But while I was stuck here, I might as well show Geraldine Jiggles she hadn't made a mistake by hiring me.

I know. I'll get this thrift shop so clean and organized, Geraldine won't know what hit her when she walks back in the place!

Feeling invigorated with purpose, I stowed my purse on the bottom shelf under the cash register and rummaged around until I found a can of Lysol.

"Now, where to start?" I said aloud. I glanced around. It didn't take long to spot a target. "Aha!" I said, then I aimed the can squarely at a dried-up puddle of mystery goo on the countertop. I mashed the spray button. Nothing came out but a dry hiss. I let out a sigh.

Figures.

With no other cleaning products to be found, I grabbed Geraldine's keys and headed for the storage room in the back. After trying half a dozen keys, I finally hit upon the right one. I opened the gray door and surveyed the shelves lining the back wall. The shelf where all J.D.'s Hummels once stood was now empty.

I grimaced with guilt. But what was done was done. I pressed on in my search for cleaning supplies.

A jumble of empty cardboard boxes cluttered the floor, blocking my view of the bottom shelf. I started to push one out of the way, then remembered Geraldine had informed me that part of my glamourous new job was to break down cartons and throw them in the dumpster out back.

Might as well get to it.

I plucked a box cutter from a hook on the wall and grabbed an empty box. Ten minutes later, I'd sliced through the packing tape on half a dozen boxes. Neatly folded, they now leaned against the door leading to the alley out back. The one in front had J.D.'s initials on it. I cringed.

J.D. and Laverne were probably at their new condo right now, unpacking. I wondered how the short, silver-haired attorney was going to react when he discovered that four boxes of his prized treasures had come up missing.

For a high-powered lawyer, J.D. was incredibly even-tempered. In fact, I'd only seen him lose his cool once. It had happened right after he'd moved in with Laverne. In an attempt to make room for his clothes in her bedroom closet, Laverne had sold five of J.D.'s custom Armani suits at the neighborhood garage sale for a grand total of fifteen dollars.

The poor man had totally lost it. I mean, who could blame him? At four feet nothing, J.D. barely came up to Laverne's elbows. Seeing the odd pair argue out in her front yard had been like watching a squirrel do battle with a Sandhill Crane.

The memory made me snicker. I crossed my fingers and said, "Good luck, Laverne." Then I got back to the task at hand—hauling the boxes out to the dumpster.

I reached down to pick up the boxes leaning against the back door. As I lifted the stack, a cockroach as big as my thumb flew up and out of the cartons. Of course, the disgusting creature made a beeline for my face.

"Aaargh!" I screeched, then dropped the boxes and fell backward onto my butt.

The nasty roach landed on the wall by the back door. I flung the box cutter at it, but missed. As it scurried toward the safety of the crack between the door and doorframe, I scrambled over to the shelving unit on my hands and knees. I grabbed a hammer off the shelf and flung it at the roach. But I missed it again.

"Ugh!" I groaned in disgust as the oversized arthropod disappeared into the crack.

I stood, picked up the hammer, and cautiously opened the door. The roach was gone. But outside in the alley was yet another pile of boxes waiting for me to break down and fold. The one closest to the door was marked J.D. It still had a layer of bubble wrap inside.

My heart fluttered.

Could some of J.D.'s stuff still be in there? I hope so!

I sprinted over to the carton and pulled away a layer of bubble wrap.

I gasped. My mind went haywire.

There was a man inside the box!

He sat crouched, knees folded to his chest, glaring up at me with bulging blue eyes!

His arms were reaching for my throat!

An involuntary shriek erupted from my lips. My arm jerked upward, then down. The man's head fell to one side as he let out a horrible groaning sound.

I stared at him in shock and disbelief. Lord help me, I'd just whacked that poor man in the head with a hammer!

"I'm sorry!" I squealed. "You scared me! What are you doing hiding in a box in the alley, anyway?"

The man didn't answer. His bulgy eyes had gone dull. They stared blankly at the sky as the last bit of air escaped his open lips like a whispered groan.

My legs turned to sand beneath me. I fell to my knees.

This can't be happening.

I just killed a man!

Chapter Nineteen

I wish I could say I acted heroically after killing that guy in the box. That I owned up to my responsibility with dignity and integrity.

But I didn't.

Instead, I panicked and tried to cover my tracks like every homicidal loser ever featured on *Forensic Files*.

After hitting the guy in the head with the hammer, I sat there on my knees, paralyzed with shock. I stared at my victim for what seemed like an eternity. Not because I wanted to—but because I couldn't will my numb, Frankenstein legs to move.

My mind whirred in offbeat rhythm to my fluttering heart. I was certain that at any moment, someone would come by and catch me in the act.

But nobody did.

After a while, life slowly returned to my limbs. When I finally managed to stand again, my heart was thumping in my throat like a bass drum. Fumbling around on stiff, paralytic legs, I put the bubble wrap back over the guy, then tossed the hammer I'd hit him with into the dumpster.

My tracks covered, I glanced up and down the alley. I couldn't believe my luck. Nobody had seen me!

I could feel the guilt already settling in as I quickly hobbled back into the thrift store. Once inside, I made a beeline for the tiny washroom to check my face in the mirror. There was no blood on it, but plenty of guilt-ridden terror.

The strong smell of ammonia helped bring me to my senses. I opened the toilet lid, expecting the worst. But it was clean. It was me who needed washing up. I'd peed my pants. *Again.*

Maybe I need to see a urologist ...

My mind still a muddle, I glanced around the store and spotted a pair of old lady bloomers.

Eww!

I snatched them from atop a pile of crumpled women's clothes. As I changed into them, the gravity of my situation began to set in.

I killed a guy. I really, actually, totally killed a guy.

My lips began to tremble uncontrollably. How was I going to get out of this? I wasn't strong enough to lift the body to hide it away in the dumpster. And I couldn't run, either. There was only $80 in the cash register. That wouldn't even buy bus fare out of Tampa.

Then a thought hit me.

What if the guy isn't completely dead? If I call now, maybe they can still save him! Oh, please, please, please don't let him be dead!

I grabbed the landline phone beside the cash register and dialed 9-1-1. When I tried to talk into the receiver, I realized my mouth was malfunctioning as badly as my brain. I could barely speak.

"D... d ... dead guy!" I stuttered into the phone.

"Calm *down*, ma'am," a voice said on the other end of the 9-1-1 line. (As if that advice ever worked on anybody.) "Speak clearly. What did you say?"

My brain bubbled like a pot of chili in a nuclear reactor. "D ... dead guy!"

"Where are you?"

My mind spun like a roulette wheel, then landed on an answer. "Uh ... St. Petersburg!"

"I meant your *street location*, ma'am."

"Uh ... Corey Avenue. Blown-up Rooms!"

"There was an explosion?"

"No. I mean ... uh ... *Belated Rooms*. Dead guy!"

"I understand there is a deceased man with you ma'am. Is he still breathing?"

WTH???

Ironically, it was the operator's inane question that snapped me partially back to my senses. "No. I mean ... I don't think so."

"Could you check?"

I grimaced. "Do I have to?"

"I need you to listen carefully to me, ma'am. Do you know who the man is?"

"No! Could you please send somebody? *Now?*"

"I've already dispatched emergency medical response. They're just a block away. Could you begin initiating CPR?"

Bile rose in my throat. "I don't know how."

"I'll walk you through it."

"Uh ... okay—"

Suddenly, the door to the thrift shop flew open. A pair of EMTs rushed inside. I slammed the phone back into the receiver.

"Back there!" I yelled, pointing a trembling finger toward the rear of the store. "He's in the alley! Through the back door!"

• • • •

THE MALE EMT SHOOK his head and dropped the guy's wrist. It fell back into the box with the rest of him. He pulled off his rubber gloves and said, "It's too late. He's gone."

"Too bad," the female EMT said. She glanced over at me. "You found him in the alley like this?"

I cringed. "Sort of. I opened the box, and he was inside."

"What's with the circular dent in his forehead?" she asked.

Panic shot through me again. "I ... uh ... have no idea. I mean, how should I know?"

The woman eyed me funny, then took a step back away from me. "I'm going to need you to calm down, ma'am."

Calm down? Are you out of your freaking gourd?

I glanced around and thought about making a run for it. The male EMT must've read my mind. He took up a position opposite his partner, effectively blocking my escape.

"Take it easy, lady," he said, eyeing me with suspicion. "The police should be here any minute."

"The police?" I gulped.

"Yes, the police," the man said. He made a quick motion with his hand, then before I knew what was happening, the pair of EMTs each grabbed one of my arms and escorted me back inside the shop.

Chapter Twenty

With strong-armed EMTs hustling me away from the scene of the crime and back into Belated Rooms, there was no denying it. My dirty little hammer habit had finally gone too far.

What had I been thinking, smashing figurines to bits? I should've known it would only lead to rack and ruin. I'd gone and turned myself into a walking hammer-homicide waiting to happen!

The EMTs sat me down in a ratty wooden rocking chair next to the plate glass window by the front door. From my vantage point, I tried to look innocent as the place filled up with uniformed police officers and stern-faced professionals in black jackets with the word *Forensics* emblazoned on the back.

How long would it take for them to point the finger at me?

I craned my neck to hear what the male EMT was saying to one of the police officers. Then I wished I hadn't.

"This looks like homicide to me, Brady," he said. "Unless the guy committed suicide by crawling into a box and beating himself to death."

The EMT and the cop both glanced over at me. Caught like a possum in a trap, I stared, wide-eyed, as the cop gave the EMT a nod, then headed right for me. My mind scrambled. Unable to think, I averted my eyes and tried to whistle. But I couldn't. I'd forgotten that I never actually could.

"You the lady who called this in?" the cop asked.

I shot a guilty glance up at him. The officer's blue eyes were studying me like a bug under a microscope. His muscular physique and boyish face reminded me of Tom. But this man was much younger. And his eyes and hair were the deep, dark brown of a double-fudge Oreo.

I wonder if they serve Oreos in prison ...

"Ma'am?" the cop said. "Did you call in this report?"

"Uh ... yes," I whispered in a strained voice.

"Pretty gruesome sight, I bet," he said.

I nodded.

"I'm Officer Brady. I heard you discovered the victim inside a cardboard box in the alley. Is that correct?"

I swallowed hard. "Yes, sir."

To my surprise, the young cop offered me a sympathetic smile. "That must've been some shock." He glanced up over my shoulder through the storefront window. Suddenly, his friendly demeanor evaporated.

A second later, the front door squealed open. "Brady!" a deep, baritone voice rang out. "Is that the one who found the body?"

Officer Brady's shoulders stiffened like an army recruit. "Yes, sir, Sergeant McNulty!"

I turned to see a tall, slim, middle-aged black man walking swiftly toward us. The sleeves of his uniform were adorned with stripes. "Are you Ms. Frendle?"

"Fremden." I smiled weakly. "It means *strangers* in German."

"Why would you tell me *that*?" McNulty pulled a small notebook from his front pocket and scribbled something into it. Whatever it was, I had the feeling it couldn't be good.

"She's just nervous, sir," the young cop named Brady said. "She just found a murder victim, after all."

McNulty's brow furrowed above his mirrored aviator sunglasses. "Brady, you're needed on perimeter patrol. *Now.* I'll take it from here."

"Yes, sir." Brady gave me a quick nod, then hustled out the front door.

"I'm Sergeant McNulty," the man said. "Would you mind telling me what you were doing here at this shop?"

I fiddled with a crocheted doily lying on the rocking chair's armrest. "I was working here, sir. This is ... *was* ... my first day on the job."

"You don't say. That's some particularly odd timing now, isn't it? When did you first arrive on the scene?"

I gulped. "The *scene?*"

"The shop. When did you get to work this morning?"

"Oh. At 8:00 a.m. sharp."

McNulty noted that down. "Were you alone?"

"No. The owner was here. Ms. Jiggles."

"*Jiggles?*" He shot me a skeptical look. "Uh-huh. And where is Ms. Jiggles now?"

"Probably somewhere over Utah. She left this morning to catch a plane to Vegas at one o'clock."

"So, you've been working alone in the shop since she left?"

"Yes. Since around 9:30."

"Right." McNulty wrote something in his notebook. "Who else works here, Ms. Fremden?"

"I dunno. Just me, I guess. There's a guy named Jerry, too. But he didn't show up yesterday, so I took his place."

McNulty's eyes narrowed. "You told me *today* was your first day on the job."

I gripped the chair's armrest to steady myself. "Uh ... first *paid* day. Yesterday I was here for training."

And tomorrow I'll be training to make license plates in Folsom Prison.

"Mm-hmm." McNulty scribbled some more. "Besides you and Ms. Jiggles, who has access to the premises?"

I grimaced. "I don't know. I guess Jerry or anybody could have a key."

"*Anybody?*" Even though McNulty's eyes were hidden behind mirrored shades, I could feel them boring into me.

"Whoever else might work here, I mean."

"Are you being willfully uncooperative, Ms. Fremden?"

The question hit me like a slap in the face. I blanched. "Uh ... no sir! I really don't know much of anything about this place. I only found out Belated Rooms even existed yesterday, when I helped a friend donate some boxes of junk."

"A friend?"

"Yes. My neighbor. Laverne Cowens."

"What kind of 'junk' was in the boxes?"

"Some old stuff of her husband J.D.'s."

McNulty's eyebrow crooked above his sunglasses. He scribbled in his notepad. "Did you at any point today leave the shop today?"

I winced. "Only to grab lunch with a friend."

"So that's a 'yes'?"

"Yes."

"What time frame?"

"From around 11:30 to 2 p.m."

He peeked at me from above his sunglasses. "Nice long lunch. Did you lock the shop door when you left?"

I doubled down on my grip on the armrest. "Uh. I don't remember for sure."

"And you found the body when you returned from lunch."

"Yes, sir."

"Any idea who the man might be?"

"No. Only maybe Jerry. I saw a picture of him once. It might be him."

"What's his last name?"

"Uh ... Kowalski or something like that."

"Tell me, Fremden. Why did you go into the alley this afternoon?"

I looked up at McNulty. "I was breaking down boxes to throw into the dumpster. It's part of my job."

"How convenient."

My heart skipped a guilty beat. "Convenient?"

"The dead man might be the thrift store employee who lost his job to you. He didn't turn up for work yesterday. Today he's found in a box behind the store. A box with the initials J.D on it—which you delivered here yourself yesterday. Do you see where I'm going with this?"

My throat went dry. "But—"

McNulty tucked his notebook into his shirt pocket. "I'm going to need you to come down to the station with me."

Oh, dear lord. He sees right through me!

"Why?" I squealed.

"To get your statement."

"About what? I just told you—"

"Ms. Fremden, we're going to need a detailed report of your exact movements during the last 24 hours."

My heart played a drum solo in my chest. Then the rocking chair arms I'd been squeezing like a vice broke off in my hands.

McNulty's eyebrow shot up. "Nervous?"

"A little." I swallowed hard. "Can I grab my purse first? It's on a shelf under the cash register over there."

McNulty shook his head. "No. I'll have an officer bring your personal effects to the station for processing."

"Processing?" I stood up. My knees wobbled. "How long will that take?"

McNulty's lips formed a grim line. "Depending on your alibi, about an hour—give or take 50 years to life."

Chapter Twenty-One

If I claimed to be unfamiliar with police interrogation rooms, that would be a lie as big as the one I was trying to pull over on Sergeant McNulty.

Since returning to St. Pete flat broke five years ago, I'd found myself on the wrong side of a cold metal table in a tiny, concrete-block room on more occasions than I cared to remember.

The reasons for me being hauled into various police stations ranged from falsifying public records to stealing a body out of a morgue to harboring a fugitive pet pig on the lam. I'd also been accused of human dismemberment and assaulting an officer's toupee (long story).

I could happily report that in every case, I'd been cleared of all charges. But this time felt different. I'd never been up against Sergeant McNulty before.

Oh, and I'd never actually been *guilty* before, either.

• • • •

"SO LET ME GET THIS straight," McNulty said. "A woman named Lily came in and told you the missing employee named Jerry owed her child support. She gave you a business card and asked you to call her if you saw him."

"Correct. That's how I know what Jerry looks like."

McNulty's eyes narrowed. "But now you can't find her business card."

"Uh ... correct."

"You also helped your friend Cowens dump off thousands of dollars' worth of Hummel figurines at the thrift shop with no thought as to remuneration. Correct?"

"Not exactly. Laverne paid me five dollars to help her."

McNulty's jaw tightened. "That's not what I meant. Why didn't Cowens sell the items instead?"

I fidgeted in my chair. "Uh ... she was in a hurry. She's moving house today. Laverne wanted the figurines to 'get lost,' so she could blame it on the movers."

"Get lost? Why?"

"Because they're ugly. Have you ever *seen* a Hummel?"

McNulty's lips puckered. "So, you don't like Hummels."

I folded my arms. "No, sir."

"I see. So, tell me, Ms. Fremden. Do you like *hammers*?"

"H ... hammers?" I stammered. McNulty had punched me in the gut again. "What do you mean?"

"The forensic crew noted multiple images of hammers on your cell phone. Hammers featured in a series of 'before and after' pictures of figurines being crushed." McNulty turned a laptop computer around so I could see the screen. "Recognize this?"

Displayed on the computer screen was the 'before' image of my latest kill. It was the chipped weightlifter figurine I'd bought off that lady with the wheelbarrow yesterday. I'd written MARCO on its forehead. I cringed.

McNulty tapped the screen. A new image appeared. The 'after' shot. The figurine was a pile of crumbled shards. On one of the pieces, I could still make out the letter M.

I glanced down at my hands. "So? Smashing figurines isn't against the law, is it?"

"No. But you appear quite adept at swinging a hammer, Ms. Fremden. That worries me, considering our victim in the box sustained quite a blow to the head. It left a mark suspiciously like the business end of a hammer."

My mouth went dry. "Really?" I squeaked. "How odd. But Officer McNulty, the pictures on my phone are just figurines. Not people."

McNulty tilted his head and locked eyes with me. "Killers often take trophy pictures, Ms. Fremden. And in the case of *serial* killers, their behaviors often escalate."

I gulped. "Escalate?"

"Yes." McNulty's eyes bore into me. "Most hone their killing skills by practicing on inanimate objects. Then they move up to more risky targets, like animals. Then humans."

"They do?"

"Yes, they do."

My heart felt like a hammer beating against my throat. Had I actually managed to lapse into the role of a serial killer? If I *had*, I wasn't going to admit it to myself. And I certainly wasn't going to tell McNulty! Taking a cue from the killers I'd watched on TV, I copped a tough attitude.

"Like I told you before. My victims are all *figurines*. Not humans. And I only use my personal hammer."

"You have a *personal* hammer?" McNulty asked.

"Yes. I'll show you." I flipped through the images on his computer until I found what I was looking for. I turned the screen to face him. "See? *My* hammer has the initials H-O-J carved into it."

McNulty raised an eyebrow. "H-O-J?"

My cheeks flared with heat. "Um ... yes. It's my Hammer of Justice."

"I see." McNulty tapped on his computer a few times, then flipped the screen back to face me. "Tell me, Fremden. Does anything here look familiar to you?"

I peered at the screen and nearly fainted. There he was. That poor, bloated, bulgy-eyed guy from the box. He was laid out on an examining table. Beside him was the cardboard carton he'd arrived in. I could see J.D.'s initials on it. And at the bottom of that box was a hammer.

A hammer with three distinct initials on the handle.

H-O-J.

I gasped. "But that's not possible!"

McNulty raised an innocent-looking eyebrow. "Why not?"

"Because the hammer I hit that guy in the head with was black and yellow," I squealed. "And I threw it in the dumpster!"

Chapter Twenty-Two

Sometimes I'd pay good money to go back in time and punch myself in the face. This was one of those times.

After the stupid confession I'd blurted, I figured my goose was well and fully cooked. Ironically, all that remained was for the real "hammer of justice" to come down again—this time on *my* head.

So much for going down in history as the criminal mastermind of the century. Given the sloppy trail I'd left, I supposed it hadn't been hard for Sergeant McNulty to sniff me out. But if I'd learned anything from watching hundreds of TV shows about cold-blooded killers, it was this; it never *ever* paid to confess.

But then again, as I sat alone in the cold dankness of the interrogation room, I knew that ship had already sailed.

• • • •

AFTER SPILLING MY OWN beans on myself, I'd hung my head and told McNulty I wanted an attorney. The interrogation over, I'd sat there in stunned silence as McNulty read me my Miranda Rights. After that, a big, burly guy in uniform appeared at the door, ready to take me on an escorted stroll to a bleak, empty holding cell.

Sitting on a hard bench inside it now, I could still hear the claustrophobic *clang* of the iron bars as they'd closed behind me. I stared blankly through the bars, knowing full well I had no one to blame but myself.

McNulty was right. Like a serial killer, I'd played with fire—until I'd finally crossed the line from ceramic skulls to flesh-and-blood ones.

Bewildered and ashamed, I put my head in my hands and burst into tears.

• • • •

I WAS STILL SOBBING when a policewoman came and unlocked the door to the holding cell.

"Fremden?" she asked.

I glanced up through my tears. "Yes?"

"Time for your one phone call. Come with me."

I stumbled behind the female cop, my legs wobbling like a newborn colt's. She led me to a small room with a table, a chair, a landline phone, and an old telephone book complete with yellow pages. It looked like a scene straight out of *Matlock*.

"I'll be back in ten minutes," the female cop said right before she closed and locked the door behind her. "Better get busy."

I stared at the phone wondering who I should call. Tom?

Hi, Tom. I know I'm not supposed to call you during your "special assignment." Just wanted to give you a heads-up in case you hear rumors around the water cooler that I killed a guy. Okay. Gotta go. Hope you have a nice life with that woman who laughed on our answering machine.

Yeah. No.

I chewed my thumbnail. What about Laverne?

Hey, Laverne. Don't tell J.D., but I kinda killed a guy hiding in one of those boxes we used to steal his Hummels. Any chance you know a thug in Vegas who can come break me out of prison?

Dicey at best. What about Milly?

Oh, hi, Milly. I just murdered somebody. Guess I won't make it to our stakeout plans at the Don Cesar tomorrow. Would you mind bringing me a toothbrush?

111

I let out a long, withering sigh. Even in my desperate, befuddled state, I knew I needed an attorney like a junkie needed an intervention. I glanced at the clock on the wall. Only five minutes left.

Think, Val. Think!

Besides the mysterious Mr. Bardsmore, I was only acquainted with two attorneys. One was an ambulance-chasing scumbag named Ferrol Finkerman. The other one was J.D. Fellows. J.D. was a ton more credible, but I'd just played accomplice to disposing of his prized possessions—and then possibly even incriminated him by murdering a man inside a box with his initials scrawled on it!

No way. Calling J.D. Fellows was out of the question.

The clock on the wall ticked down to three minutes. As I wracked my brain trying to think of who to call, a thought stopped me cold.

What if I call someone and get their answering machine? Will that be it? Will my one and only call be done? Or will they give me a do-over?

That's when I knew who I would call. The only person I knew desperate enough to answer a call from a prison inmate. Ferrol Finkerman.

God help me!

With trembling hands, I picked up the phone, swallowed what dignity I had left, and made the call.

"It's a fine day for a Finkerman," his nasally voice whined.

My gut churned with instant regret. "Uh ... wrong number."

"Fremden? Is that you?"

I cringed. "Uh ... yeah."

He let out a short laugh. "What'd you do this time? Wait! Let me guess. Harboring a fugitive ferret? Mangling another trooper's hideous hairpiece?"

"No. Just murder, plain and simple. Bye."

"Hold on!" he yelled. "Murder? What happened?"

"Never mind. It was a mistake to call you."

I clicked off the phone and grabbed the phone book. I rifled through the hundred-plus pages of attorneys. How was I supposed to pick one out of all this sea of inhumanity?

I glanced at the clock. Fourteen seconds left. I closed my eyes and let the breath go out of me like a deflating balloon.

I'm doomed.

Chapter Twenty-Three

What in the world was wrong with me? I'd not only gone and killed a guy—I'd then called Ferrol Finkerman and told him all about it!

That's it. I must be crazy. That's the only plausible explanation.

I let out a groan. Then I slumped against the cold concrete wall of my holding cell. I began to wonder if I beat my head against the wall if it would knock some sense into me. Knowing myself, probably not.

But at least I hadn't stooped so low as to hire that ambulance chaser Ferrol Finkerman. Having him as my attorney would be worse than me representing myself—and I'd just officially declared myself *insane.*

Still, getting rid of Finkerman had only eliminated one moron from the equation. There was still one left.

Me.

• • • •

AN HOUR AGO, THE POLICEWOMAN had come and taken me back to my cell. I'd begged her to let me have another call, but she'd only given me a dubious look and said she'd ask her supervisor. I hadn't heard a word since then.

The chances I'd get another call were fading by the second. What should I have expected? Given what I'd done to that poor guy in the box, I didn't deserve another chance.

I was busy gnawing my thumbnail to the quick when a movement caught my eye. Through the holding cell bars, I spotted that same policewoman coming toward me. Keys were dangling from her hand. My heart began thumping in my chest.

She unlocked the cell door. I crossed my fingers and hoped she wasn't coming back to do a strip search.

"Okay, Fremden. Come with me." She led me down the hallway to the phone room. "You got ten minutes. That's it. Got it?"

My heart soared. "Oh, thank you so much, ma'am!"

"*Ma'am?*" Her expression soured. "I'm younger than you."

I cringed. "Sorry! I meant to say, 'officer.'"

She grabbed my arm and shoved me into the room. "Ten minutes and not a second more."

I tumbled inside and was startled to find I wasn't alone in the tiny room. Seated at the desk was a tall, thin, beady-eyed man with thinning, frizzy red hair. He was wearing a pale-blue polyester leisure suit harboring at least five decades worth of accumulated stains.

"Finkerman!" I gasped. "What are *you* doing here?"

"I believe the real question is, Fremden, what are *you* doing here?"

Finkerman's pathetic wad of reddish hair defied physics, appearing both greasy and frizzy at the same time. He'd carefully pasted the floppy mess across his bulbous, shiny dome, creating one of the world's most obvious comb-overs.

"This guy says he's your attorney," the policewoman said, eyeing him up and down. "Is that true? Or is he some kind of pervy uncle of yours?"

I grimaced. "Uh ... he's my attorney, I guess."

She shook her head. "Well, all I can say is, heaven help you, lady."

• • • •

"I ALWAYS KNEW THIS day would come," Finkerman said, rubbing his boney, freckled hands together. His narrow, pasty face twisted into a ghastly smirk. "When the times get tough, they always come crawling back to Finkerman."

"You talking clients or body lice?" I asked as I sat down across the table from him. I scooted my chair further away, just in case he'd meant the latter.

Finkerman's smirk soured. "Real funny, Fremden. You want my help or not?"

I grimaced. "Okay. Fine. You see, it all started—"

Finkerman held an open palm up to my face like a stop sign. "Hold that thought." He handed me a clipboard. "Sign this paper before you say another word."

I frowned at the clipboard. "What is it? Your confidentiality agreement?"

"Huh? Oh, sure. It's also a contract agreeing to my retainer. I need $357.45 up front to represent you."

My nose crinkled. "That seems like an awfully specific amount."

Finkerman shrugged. "Yeah, I thought so, too. But that's what it costs nowadays to replace the timing belt on a 1974 AMC Gremlin."

Chapter Twenty-Four

"And that's when I opened the box and found the guy hiding inside," I said to Finkerman. I swallowed hard, not wanting my next words to spill out. They did anyway.

"I ... panicked!" I wrung my hands. "Before I even realized what I was doing, I hit the guy between the eyes with a hammer! I didn't mean to. It was ... a ... a ... *reflex action!*"

Finkerman studied me, his expression more curious than judgmental. "Where'd you get the hammer?"

I stopped wringing my hands and stared at him.

That's your only question about all of this?

"From a shelf in the storeroom," I said. "Why?"

He pursed his lips. "You're telling me you had the presence of mind to go grab the hammer off the shelf before this man overtook you?"

I shook my head. "No. I already had the hammer in my hand when I went out in the alley and opened the box."

Finkerman nodded and rubbed his freckled chin. "So, you knew the man was in the box. And you brought the hammer with you as protection? To defend yourself?"

"Not exactly." I felt a bead of sweat trickle down my back. Was it this stuffy little room we were locked in, or was it the fires of hell heating up to fry my guilty ass?

"No," I said. "I didn't know the guy was hiding in the box."

Finkerman frowned. "I don't get it, Fremden. What were you doing with a hammer in your hand?"

I cringed. "I was trying to kill a roach with it. In the storeroom at the back of the shop."

"I see." Finkerman's brow furrowed. Then, all of a sudden, his expression took on a sly look, as if some dim-wattage light bulb had gone off inside his pathetic noggin. "Tell me. Did said roach at any time begin to fly?"

"Huh?" I grunted. "Well, yeah. It flew right at me. But what's that got to—"

"Aha!" Finkerman's pasty face lit up. "That's it!"

I blanched. "What are you talking about?"

"Trapped alone in a room with a flying cockroach? Come on, Fremden. That's the very *definition* of temporary insanity! Anybody who lives in Florida knows that."

A tiny spark of hope flickered inside me. "So, you think I could plead—"

"You were acting on impulse, brought on by hysteria," Finkerman said, nodding to himself. His gleaming, beady eyes met mine. "It's elementary, Fremden."

"What is?"

"You were out of your mind with primal fear, that's what! You naturally grabbed the nearest thing you could find to defend yourself. Right?"

"Right." I grimaced. "Except ..."

Finkerman frowned. "Except *what*?"

"The hammer they found in the box with the dead guy wasn't the one I hit him with."

Finkerman grinned. "Even better! You never handled the murder weapon!"

I cringed. "That's not exactly right, either."

"Geez, Fremden. Don't tell me you picked this other hammer up!"

I shook my head. "No. Even worse. You see, the hammer they found in the box is *mine*. It has my initials on it."

Finkerman's face fell like an anvil off a cliff. "Aww, crap. You brought the murder weapon with you to your workplace?" He shook his head. "Not good, Fremden. Not good at all."

"But that's just it. I *didn't*."

"Then just exactly how did your personal hammer get to the thrift shop? Flying monkeys?"

I blew out a breath and shook my head. "I honestly don't have any idea."

Finkerman glanced around, then leaned across the table and whispered, "You're covered by client confidentiality, okay? Be real with me. Are you on crack or something?"

"No!"

"Okay, okay! Geez. Take it easy, Fremden." Finkerman tugged at his shirt collar. "I was just checking. It's called due diligence, okay?"

"Okay. Sorry."

"Think, Fremden. Who else could've brought *your* personal hammer to Belated Rooms?"

I shook my head. "I dunno."

"Well, you better think of who, and fast. Transporting a murder weapon to a crime scene implies *premeditation*. That blows our temporary insanity defense right out the window."

My heart dropped. "But I never planned to kill the guy. I swear! It was an accident! I don't even know who he is!"

Suddenly, the door to the tiny phone room flew open. Sergeant McNulty stuck his head inside. "Time's up."

"But we haven't finished!" I pleaded.

"Don't worry, Fremden," Finkerman said. "Hopefully, they'll go easy on you, considering this is your first offense. This *is* your first murder, isn't it?"

I glanced at Finkerman, then up at McNulty. What was I supposed to say to *that*?

"Well, I guess I best get going," Finkerman said. "Listen, Fremden. A little free advice. If you *have* done other murders besides this one, don't tell ..." He glanced over at McNulty. "Well, you know who."

"Thanks," I muttered between gritted teeth. If a cop hadn't been there to bear witness to assault, I'd have kicked Finkerman in the groin.

In a flash of pale-blue polyester, Finkerman squirmed past McNulty and out of the room. The sergeant turned to face me. "Don't tell me that guy's your attorney."

I hung my head. "Okay. I won't tell you."

Chapter Twenty-Five

I squinted through my guilty tears at the hazy outline of Sergeant McNulty towering above me. I was still sitting at the table Finkerman had just vacated. All that was left of him was the lingering odor of his cheap cologne.

"Get up, Fremden," McNulty said.

"Yes, sir."

I stood and held my hands out to be cuffed. "What happens now?"

McNulty studied me with his raven-black eyes until I started to squirm. Finally, he said, "You're free to go."

My knees buckled. I had to grab the table to keep from hitting the floor.

"I *am*?" I asked.

"You heard me."

I swallowed hard. "But a couple of hours ago, you said I'd never see the light of day again."

McNulty let out a tired sigh. "That was before some new evidence came to light."

I forced a weak smile. "New evidence?"

"Yes. According to the preliminary coroner's report, the victim was dead *before* you hit him in the head with the hammer."

"He was?" Suddenly, my head felt like a helium balloon. I flopped back into the chair. "So ... I didn't kill the guy?"

"There was no bleeding or bruising present around the hammer strike you said you inflicted today," McNulty said. "The initial report indicated the victim's been dead at least 24 hours."

I felt light as air, as if I might float to the ceiling.

I'm not a murderer! This is all over, and none of my friends and family ever have to know a thing about it!

I practically swooned with relief. "Thank you, Sergeant McNulty! So, I'm officially off the hook?"

"I wouldn't say that," McNulty said. "The findings only clear you of your confession of killing the man *today*. Who's to say you didn't kill him yesterday?"

My mouth fell open. "But ... I didn't kill him yesterday, either! If I had, why on earth would I pretend to kill him again today?"

"In an amateur move to cover your tracks," McNulty said, not missing a beat. "Or do you have a plausible explanation as to how your personal 'Hammer of Justice' came to be in the box with the victim?"

I gulped. "No. I don't know. Somebody else must've put it there." I thought back to yesterday and gasped. "I couldn't find it yesterday. You know, when I smashed that bodybuilder figurine. Somebody must've broken into my garage and stolen it!"

"Sure," McNulty said. "We've had a rash of hammer thefts lately."

My eyes grew wide. "You have?"

"Of course not!" McNulty scowled. "It's far more likely that you killed this man with your hammer yesterday, then returned to the scene of the crime this morning to retrieve your murder weapon. But you couldn't find it, so you hit him with another hammer to try and throw us off your track."

"If I wanted to throw you off my track, why would I call 9-1-1 and report finding him?"

"Criminals do it all the time."

I thought back to those investigation programs on TV. McNulty wasn't lying. Criminals weren't always what you'd call "masterminds."

I cringed. "Look. I swear I didn't kill him. Why would I? I don't even know him. And besides, I'm not that strong. How could I have gotten him into that box in the alley in the first place?"

"With an accomplice."

I nearly gasped. "*Accomplice*?"

McNulty studied me for a moment, then motioned for me to stand. "Look, Ms. Fremden. Lucky for you, in America you're still innocent until proven guilty. In your case, I'm just going to have to work a little harder to prove it."

"But—"

He opened the door to the tiny room. "You're free to go while we conduct our investigation. But one slip up from you and you're right back in here for abuse of a corpse. Got it?"

I swallowed hard. "Yes, sir. Got it."

• • • •

THANK GOODNESS FOR that whole "innocent until proven guilty" thing. Sergeant McNulty had let me go—with the caveat that I didn't leave town.

Like an injured sea turtle being set free after recovery, I rushed out the door of the police station. As I sprinted through the lobby, I ducked my head in hopes I wouldn't be spotted by my boyfriend, Tom. When I made it out the door and into the blessed sunshine, I felt like that guy who escaped in *The Shawshank Redemption*.

I was scurrying around the corner of the building in a race to put some distance between me and a jail cell when I ran headlong into the arms of Ferrol Finkerman.

"Ugh! What are you still doing here?" I asked, pushing myself off him and his dingy polyester suit.

"I was coming back in to see you."

I glanced down at my blouse to check for transfer stains, then glared at him. "Why?"

"You still owe me my retainer."

"Are you serious?" I didn't have enough money for a cab ride home, much less to pay lowlife Finkerman. "Okay, fine. Give me a ride back to the thrift shop and I'll give you your money."

Finkerman glanced around the parking lot. "Wait. How'd you get out? I'm not harboring a fugitive, am I?"

123

"You're worried about your reputation? That's rich." I rolled my eyes. "I'm not on the lam. McNulty let me go. Now give me a ride. I'll explain along the way."

• • • •

FINKERMAN JIGGLED THE keys in the ignition of his orange Gremlin and uttered some magical set of curse words until it finally coughed to life. As we rolled out of the police station parking lot, I covered my face with my hands. I didn't want to be caught dead in a Gremlin *or* with Finkerman.

"I still can't believe that McNulty guy let you go," Finkerman said. "Sure looked to me like he had it in for you."

"Maybe. But Tom told me he's new to the squad. New guys always have a lot to prove."

"Like your guilt?"

I scowled. "No. He *can't*. I'm innocent, remember?"

Finkerman shot me a hard glance. "If you say so. But if you're being square with me, that only leaves one other option. Somebody's trying to frame you for the murder."

I blanched. "Frame me?"

"Oldest trick in the book, Fremden. You know anybody who'd profit from getting you out of the picture?"

I grimaced.

Do I know anyone who wouldn't?

I went down the list in my head. Did Tom's new answering machine girlfriend want to eliminate the competition? Was that guy Jerry sore at me for taking his job at Belated Rooms? What about Bardsmore? Or Marco? Could J.D. be getting even with me for helping dispose of his precious Hummels? Or is this a revenge job by some random shopkeeper who went out of business after Tiffany's Temp sent me to work for them?

Geez. I didn't realize how popular I was—for all the wrong reasons.

"You're either drawing a blank or compiling a horde of suspects as long as Santa's naughty list," Finkerman said.

I chewed my bottom lip. Maybe Finkerman wasn't as dumb as he looked.

"Okay," he said. "I'll help you narrow down the suspects. Let's start with an eye for an eye. You assault anybody lately?"

I started to shout "No!" at Finkerman when I realized I actually *had* had a little run-in with someone. "Uh ... yeah. This guy Melvin Fenster. A couple of days ago, I hit him over the head with a pizza pan."

Finkerman pulled up to a traffic light and rubbed his chin. "Hmm. I've heard of lamer reasons to frame someone for murder. Anybody else spring to mind?"

I glanced out the window and nearly groaned out loud. Someone else was springing to mind, all right. Marco Shamway. There he was, lying naked in bed on that blasted billboard. The sexy, rich-as-Rockefeller twit looked down his perfect nose at me while here I sat, flat broke, in a rusted-out Gremlin with a skinny, pasty-faced shyster in a polyester leisure suit.

Life is so unfair.

I pointed a finger at the billboard. "Well, it's a longshot. But that guy Marco Shamway stole my idea for the Hunk Clock."

Finkerman looked up at the sign and launched into a coughing fit. After nearly choking to death, he managed to sputter, "You mean that guy on the billboard?"

I scowled and crossed my arms. "Yeah. If I could prove the Hunk Clock was my idea, he'd probably owe me like ... a million dollars or something."

A horn honked. Finkerman hit the gas. His beady eyes homed in on me like a starving bird of prey. "As your attorney, my money's on Shamway being the culprit."

I shot him a dirty look. "I *bet* it is."

Finkerman put a hand to his chest as if I'd just offended him. "I only have your best interests at heart, Fremden. Seriously. Has Shamway been in touch with you?"

I sighed. "No. But yesterday, some attorney came by my house and stuck his business card on my door. I don't know what he wants, but it could be about Shamway."

"What's the guy's name?"

"Bloodworth, or something like that. He was driving a red Ferrari."

Finkerman's eyes narrowed. "Anthony Bardsmore?"

My eyebrows rose an inch. "Yeah. That's it. You know him?"

"I've heard his name in certain circles."

"Oh yeah? What kind? Circle-J convenience stores?"

"Excuse *me*," Finkerman huffed. "But on a hot day like today, nobody can beat a Circle-J kiwi Bluster."

I crinkled my nose. "Bluster? What is that? Some kind of disease from down under?"

Finkerman frowned and shook his head. "What planet have you been living on? It's a slushie. You know. Like an Icee or a Slurpee. I'm telling you, the kiwi flavor will change your world."

I scowled. "I'm kind of busy trying to change my world in another way. As in *not going to prison for murder*. Remember?"

"Sure. But that doesn't mean you can't stop into a Circle-J and enjoy a nice, ice-cold Bluster along the way."

I shook my head. "Whatever. Seriously, Finkerman. What do you think this attorney Bardsmore wants from me?"

Finkerman laughed sullenly. "My guess? Everything but your soul, Fremden."

I sneered at him. "I guess you should know."

Finkerman smirked. "Come on. We're not *all* that way. Why do you think I'm driving a 1974 Gremlin?"

I shrugged. "I dunno. Maybe because you've already sold your soul for a kiwi Bluster?"

Chapter Twenty-Six

A guy driving a three-wheeler dune buggy blew past us on Gulf Boulevard. Finkerman pounded the horn on his Gremlin. It let out an anemic wail like a dying antelope. He shook his fist and called the driver an uncharitable name.

"Gee. I didn't know everyone in Florida was named Dick," I said. "You know, Finkerman, you really need to get a handle on your road rage."

Finkerman let out a sarcastic laugh. "That's rich, coming from someone who just graduated from figurine smasher to serial killer. Let's see. What should we call *you*, Fremden? I know. S-H-K. Stalk, Hammer, Kill."

I frowned. "I thought you were supposed to be on *my* side."

"Oh, yeah." Finkerman wagged his eyebrows. "Right."

I watched out the passenger window as the guy in the dune buggy pulled into a Circle-J parking lot. He hopped out and joined the long line of other horndogs waiting to buy a hotdog from a cart manned by a woman in a bikini. I thought about Laverne and wondered if this was some kind of crazy sign from the universe. And if so, what the heck was it?

Giving up on solving that mystery, I turned back to the one at hand. "So, Finkerman. What do you know about this Anthony Bardsmore guy?"

"You hungry?" Finkerman asked, eyeing the scantily clad hotdog cart woman.

"No!" I hissed. "Bardsmore. Spill it!"

"Fine!" Finkerman shrugged. "He's a bigshot lawyer, apparently."

"How do you know that?"

"Any attorney who drives a Ferrari didn't get there by frying minnows like you, Fremden."

I chewed my bottom lip. "I guess you're right."

Finkerman steered his Gremlin onto Corey Avenue. Like a kid being dropped off at school by her funny uncle, I didn't want to be seen with him.

"Let me off at the corner here," I said when we were a few blocks away from Belated Rooms.

"No way." Finkerman reached over and patted my thigh, sending shivers of heebie-jeebies racing up my spine. "I'm a full-service attorney. I wouldn't want my client getting heat stroke now, would I?"

My upper lip snarled. "You're not fooling me. You're just after a cut of my million dollars."

Finkerman shot me a smarmy smile. "And what's so wrong with that? Without me, you'd never *get* the million dollars."

I crossed my arms. The jerk had a point.

"Tell you what, Fremden. Let me rep you on the Hunk Clock case, and I'll waive my retainer fee for the whole dead-guy-in-a-box thing."

Seeing as how I didn't have two nickels to pay Finkerman, I didn't exactly have much to lose. "Fine. But first, let's focus on getting me out of a murder rap, okay?"

"Of course."

Finkerman pulled his rusty old Gremlin up beside my rusty old Falcon. I climbed out.

"Call that Bardsmore guy for me," I said, handing him his business card. "Find out what he wants from me."

Finkerman tipped an imaginary hat. "First order of business, Fremden. I'll make the call right after I get home."

I glanced at all the junk stuffed in the backseat of the Gremlin. "You mean you're not actually living in this thing?"

Finkerman shrugged. "Not as far as you know."

"Great." I shook my head and unlocked the door on my old Falcon.

"Oh!" Finkerman called out. "How'd you leave it with the police?"

"McNulty told me to stay available for further interviews."

"In other words, don't leave town."

"Pretty much."

"Well, heed their advice, okay?"

"No problem." Like, where else was I gonna go with $3.27 left to my name?

I watched Finkerman disappear down the road in a cloud of dingy white smoke. The sun was setting, turning the sky a bloody gray. I shot a guilty glance up and down Corey Avenue. For once, I was grateful the old business hub was a virtual ghost town.

The shops were all closed, so there was no one around to see me as I scrambled into my car and slunk behind the steering wheel. So far, besides Finkerman and McNulty, nobody knew anything about me being accused of murder. Hopefully, it would stay that way. To make that happen, all I had to do was figure out who killed the guy in the box.

I turned the ignition on Shabby Maggie and peeled out of the parking space in front of Belated Rooms. I winced at the yellow crime-scene tape still crisscrossing the front door. The only splash of color on the dismal thrift shop, it fluttered in my wake as I sped off.

I glanced back in the rearview mirror, hoping this whole incident had just been a bad dream. But no, the telltale yellow tape was still there, flapping in the breeze.

According to Sergeant McNulty, the store would be cleared to reopen for business tomorrow, once all the crime scene prints and pictures had been taken.

It all seemed so odd. Tomorrow, the sun would rise in the east. The birds would chirp. Laverne and J.D. would wake up in their new condo. And life would return to normal for everyone ... except the dead guy in the box.

And *me*.

• • • •

129

AS I CRUISED ALONG Gulf Boulevard past the twilight glow of neon signs advertising mom-and-pop beach motels and kitschy tourist shops, the weight of my uncertain fate pressed down hard upon my shoulders.

I'm free for now, but for how long?

Even though my hammer blow this morning wasn't what had done that poor guy in, McNulty was still pointing the finger squarely at me. Given the evidence, I could hardly blame him.

I glanced at my reflection in the rearview mirror and pursed my lips.

Who hits someone in the head with a hammer? A psycho, that's who! And my excuse? Temporary insanity due to an airborne cockroach?

Even *I* knew that was one alibi that was never going to fly. Frustrated, I punched the gas pedal. Over the thunderous roar of Maggie's twin glasspack mufflers, I let out an anguished scream.

What am I supposed to do now?

As if on cue, a glowing sign beckoned me in the night. I hit the brakes and pulled a sharp right into the parking lot, tires squealing. I fished round in my purse and pulled out my only credit card. Then I climbed out of the car, praying my card balance was good for another $4.29.

By some miracle, it *was*.

After paying the clerk, I headed out the door, feeling a tiny bit lighter as I took a deep draw on the straw sticking out of my first-ever kiwi Bluster.

It didn't change my world like Finkerman had promised. But then again, it didn't make it any worse, either.

Chapter Twenty-Seven

I woke to the sound of distant ringing in my ears. I cracked open an eye, then tried to yawn.

Oddly, I couldn't. My lips were stuck together.

What the?

I tried to scream, but only managed a muffled squeal.

Help! Somebody's duct-taped my mouth shut! I'm being kidnapped!

I shot up in bed. My fingers fumbled for my lips. There was no tape across my mouth. Still, my lips wouldn't open.

Dear lord! Has somebody glued my lips together?

My mind raced. Who would do such a thing? Marco? Had he sent some goon to seal my lips so I couldn't spill the beans on how he was ripping me off?

I bolted to the bathroom and flipped on the light switch. My reflection in the vanity mirror made me let out another muffled, closed-mouth squeal.

My lips were moldy green—and my mouth tasted like rotten eggs and Elmer's glue!

Marco's poisoned me! I'm dying from the inside out!

I snatched a damp washcloth from the tub and wiped it across my gangrenous lips. To my surprise, some of the color rubbed off onto the terrycloth. I scrubbed harder. The crusty seal on my lips began to dissolve.

"What is this stuff?" I muttered through half-glued lips.

I pushed my tongue between my lips to try and moisten the gunk gluing them together. I nearly gasped at my own reflection. My tongue was avocado green, too!

What the hell is going on?

I glanced down at my feet, half expecting them to have transformed into three-toed frog flippers. They hadn't. And I instantly knew why.

There, lying in the bathroom wastebasket was my answer—a quart-sized Circle-J Bluster cup. I winced, dragged my eyes back up to my reflection in the mirror, and shook my head at my own stupidity.

Good grief. I look like I just French-kissed an iguana.

The landline in the kitchen rang. I took a step toward the hallway, but the phone only rang that one time and quit. I padded into the kitchen. The message light on my landline was blinking. I punched the play button, then reached into the cupboard for a coffee filter.

Tom's voice on the recording stopped me cold.

Hey Val. Just checking in. I've still got a lot going on here. I may not be back as soon as I thought. How'd your appointment at Tiffany's Temps go? Anything new and exciting? Uh ... gotta go. Tell you what. I'll call and let it ring once, just to let you know I'm okay. Bye.

The recorder clicked off. I scowled. I'd missed Tom's call *again*. As I fumbled angrily with the coffee filters, I took consolation in the fact that at least *this* time his message hadn't ended with some floozy giggling in the background.

• • • •

EVEN CREST WHITE STRIPS didn't make a dent on the hideous green stains still splotching my lips and tongue. With no other solution springing to mind, I tried gargling with a couple of squeezes from a ketchup bottle. (Tomatoes contain acid, right?)

That dumb idea not only failed—I choked and went into a spectacular coughing fit. After barely surviving that, I realized I had a job to get to at Belated Rooms. Begrudgingly, I showered, got dressed, and slathered my lips with thick red lipstick. Then I headed out the door, praying I wouldn't have to talk to any customers today.

Like pretty much all my other wishes, that one wasn't granted either. When I arrived at the thrift store, the cops were still there, milling about. I recognized the young cop Officer Brady. He was tearing the yellow crime tape off the front door.

I covered my mouth with my hand and called out from my car, "Should I come back later?"

"No. We're about finished up here, Ms. Fremden. You can open for business in a couple of minutes."

Crap.

"Uh ... okay, thanks."

I hit the switch to raise the ragtop on Shabby Maggie, then turned off the ignition and climbed out. As I shuffled reluctantly toward the front door of the shop, Brady waved at me with a clipboard.

"Have a good day," he said, then turned to walk down the sidewalk.

"Wait. What are you doing?" I asked.

He stopped and turned back to face me. "Interviewing the other shop owners and employees. You know. To see if they saw anything suspicious yesterday."

"Oh."

The handsome cop smiled at me. "Don't look so glum. I promise we'll get to the bottom of this."

I nearly blanched with surprise. "You don't think *I* did it?"

He shrugged. "Well, I can't rule you out completely. But I've got my suspicions you're not the killer."

I stood a little taller. "You *do*? I mean, thanks. Why?"

"Well, two things. One, I've never seen a killer look as shocked as you did yesterday. Either you're innocent or the best actress since Meryl Streep."

I smiled. "And the other reason?"

"I refuse to believe a woman who drinks kiwi Blusters would be capable of pulling off a murder."

I cringed and covered my mouth with my hand. "You noticed, eh?"

He nodded. "Of course. I notice everything. Ms. Fremden, I think if *you* were guilty of this murder, you'd have left a trail even an idiot could follow."

"Gee. Thanks—I think."

"You're welcome. Now, I better get busy. Have a nice day!"

"Right. You, too."

Officer Brady headed down the sidewalk. I stumbled into Belated Rooms feeling strangely disconcerted. The young cop seemed willing to give me the benefit of a doubt. But not Sergeant McNulty. According to *him*, I'd already left enough breadcrumbs around to stuff a Thanksgiving turkey.

And I had an awful feeling he was about to turn up the heat.

Chapter Twenty-Eight

It was hard to believe, but as I entered Belated Rooms I found the place in a state even worse than the one *I* was in. The police investigation had left an aftermath of scattered junk on the floors. Worse yet, smeary dregs of fingerprint dust covered the already grungy doors, walls, and Plexiglass check-out station.

Geez. Good thing I didn't get very far cleaning the place yesterday.

I shuffled through the debris and over to the cash register. I opened it and breathed a sigh of relief. The measly $75 Geraldine had supplied me with to run the place was still there. Good thing, as I didn't have a penny to replace it with.

I slammed the drawer with a *ching*. The small rush of wind sent a piece of paper fluttering to the floor. I picked it up. Scrawled in childish handwriting were the words:

Abandon hope, all ye who enter here.

Was that meant to be a prophecy? A warning? A clue?

For a second, I thought about handing the note over to the cops as evidence. But after a quick glance around the place, I threw it in the trash instead. Honestly, that dire warning could've been written by anyone who'd ever had the misfortune of walking into this godforsaken place.

• • • •

I WAS STANDING UNDERNEATH the thrift shop's ragged awning sweating into my plastic sandals. I had my eye on a guy across the street wielding a long pole. He was changing the sign on the movie theater. *Paradise Lost* had been plucked away letter by letter, and was now being replaced by a new flick called *That Time I Kinda ...*

Kinda what? Got my mouth tie-dyed by a kiwi Bluster?

A horn honked twice. I looked down the road and spotted Milly headed my way in her shiny red Beemer. It had taken me all morning just to clean up the shop's check-out counter. The rest of Belated Rooms still looked as if a keg of gunpowder had detonated inside it.

To keep Milly from seeing the police's crime scene handiwork, I'd risked sunstroke by waiting for her outside the shop. As she was about to pull up in front of me, I picked off a small piece of yellow crime tape still clinging to the front door. I balled the sticky wad between my fingers and flicked it onto the sidewalk out of Milly's view.

So far, my best friend had no idea about the dead guy in the alley—or that I was a prime suspect in his demise.

I needed to keep it that way.

If Milly found out, she'd probably crumble into a hysterical mess. I couldn't have that. I loved her too much. Plus, without Tom's wallet around to pick for a payday loan, I was too broke to afford gas for Shabby Maggie. I needed Milly in good enough form to be able to function as both my driver *and* stakeout partner.

"You ready to go?" Milly asked, waving at me from the driver's window of the BMW.

"Absolutely!" I left the shade of the awning and sprinted for the passenger door. I climbed inside. "Thanks for driving."

Milly's smile collapsed. "What's happened?"

My gut flopped. Did she know about the investigation? I glanced at the shop, then back to Milly. "Uh ... nothing. Why?"

"Your tongue is green!"

I nearly fainted with relief. "Oh. That? It's nothing. Long story. Funny, even. I'll tell you on the way. Let's get going."

Milly studied me, her hand frozen on the gear shift. "You promise it's not contagious?"

I laughed a bit too loudly. "I promise."

"Okay." Milly reversed out of the parking spot and hit the gas. "I hope we find Marco today. I can't wait to catch that jerk's confession on my cell phone!"

"I'd settle for just not being caught myself," I muttered.

"What was that?"

I grimaced. "Nothing."

Milly shot me a doe-eyed look of concern. "You sure you're okay, Val?"

I nodded. "Never better. Except for the green tongue, of course. It's from a Bluster."

"A what?"

"Like a slushie. Only more ... uh ... *permanent.*"

Milly shook her head. "Only you, Val."

"I know. Right?"

Milly laughed. "Okay, then. Off to the Don Cesar?"

"Yep. Let's roll."

• • • •

AS WE ARRIVED AT THE famous pink castle by the Gulf, a red Ferrari pulled out of the parking lot and sped by us in the other direction.

"Geez," I said, turning my head to follow the blur of red. "I bet that's that attorney guy."

"What attorney guy?" Milly asked.

"Anthony Bardsmore. He left his card on my door."

Her nose crinkled. "What does *he* want?"

"I dunno."

Milly wagged her head at me. "Don't tell me you're in some kind of trouble."

"Okay. I won't tell you."

"Val!"

"Next!" a man's voice called out. A suntanned arm began waving at us from the window of the Don Cesar's parking booth.

Milly shot me a frown, then pulled her BMW up to the booth window. Inside sat the same squirrely little lot

137

attendant we'd spoken with yesterday. Milly passed him her credit card.

"We'll only be here an hour or two," she said.

He glanced at her name on the card. "Got it, Ms. Halbert. You two back for more fun in the sun, I see."

"Well, yes and no," Milly said. "Could you tell me? Is Anthony Bardsmore staying here?"

The lot attendant peered at Milly over his sunglasses. "Our guests' privacy is important to us, ma'am."

"Well, was that his red Ferrari that just left?" I asked.

He shrugged. "I couldn't say. But you might have better luck asking Thonii at reception. He—"

"Save your spiel," I said. "We know the drill."

The young guy lowered his sunglasses further and took a closer look at me. He blinked twice, then winced. "Geez, lady," he said. "Have you seen anybody about that tongue?"

• • • •

"IT'S NOT THAT BAD," Milly said, inspecting my stuck-out tongue as we walked toward the poolside tiki bar at the Don Cesar. "That kid was probably just referring to your sarcastic remarks."

I frowned. "I'm not sarcastic."

"Seriously?" Milly grinned and stepped up to the bar. "That's it, Val. That Bluster thing isn't to blame. I say your tongue turned green from *lying*."

"Ha ha." I sat down in the barstool next to her and put a hand over my mouth. "You do the ordering."

"Try lemons," the cocktail waitress said, handing me a plate of wedges. It was our pal Jeri from yesterday.

"What for?" I asked.

"To get rid of that green tongue. What did you drink? Swamp juice?"

I frowned. "No. Will lemons work?"

Jeri shrugged. "They do for blue daiquiris."

"Worth a shot." I popped a lemon wedge into my mouth. My lips puckered like a puritan in a public outhouse.

Milly smirked. "I know. Jeri, we'll have two blue daiquiris, please."

Jeri grinned. "Coming right up."

I spit the lemon wedge into my hand and stuck my tongue out. "Is it working yet?"

Milly glanced at it and grimaced. "Give it another minute."

"Jeri, have you seen Marco?" I asked, then popped the lemon wedge back into my mouth.

She shook her head and poured some blue stuff into a blender. "No. Sorry."

"How about Anthony Bardsmore?" Milly asked.

Jeri stopped scooping ice into the blender and studied us. "I gotta ask: are you gals detectives or hookers?"

Milly gasped. I choked on my lemon wedge.

"Neither," I said, spitting out the slice of lemon. "It's just that ... uh ... these guys owe me money."

"Oh," Jeri said. She hit the button on the blender. "Well, sorry. Either way, I can't help you. Maybe you should just look around the pool area?"

"That's the problem," I said. "We don't exactly know what Bardsmore looks like."

"Doesn't matter," Jeri said, pouring the blue contents of the blender into two bar glasses. "Even if you could describe him, look around. All these old rich dudes look the same. I have to keep a cheat sheet to remember their names."

"A cheat sheet?" Milly asked.

"Yeah." Jeri set the daiquiris on the bar in front of us, then pulled a little notebook from her back pocket and showed it to us. In it, she'd drawn a rough sketch of the pool, and written names in little blocks all around it.

I noticed one of the names was Don M. "Is that Don McLester, the guy from yesterday?"

"Same one," Jeri said.

I shook my head. "Why is it that a fat wallet usually comes along with a fat gut and an ugly face?"

Milly sighed. "There ought to be a law against it."

Jeri laughed. "I know, right? But I have to say that Marco guy was the exception to the rule." Jeri glanced past us toward the pool. Her smile disappeared. "Don't look now, but, here comes Don the Molester in the ugly flesh."

Disobeying Jeri's order, I whirled around on my stool. Don McLester was definitely heading our way. His naked belly was bouncing between the gap of his unbuttoned Hawaiian shirt like a hairy slab of milk-colored Jell-O.

"Ugh," I groaned, then grabbed Milly by the elbow. "Come on. Let's go try Marco's room again."

"I'll keep your drinks for you in the cooler," Jeri said. "Come back and give me a full report. Especially if you punch him in the face or something."

Milly appeared confused. "But who's going to talk to Don?"

Jeri sighed. "I'll take one for the team."

Chapter Twenty-Nine

After narrowly escaping Don McLester and his Belly of Libido Death, Milly and I snuck up to the second floor of the Don Cesar and were back at Marco's door, room number 22.

I banged on the door six times with no answer. Lucky number seven didn't work either. Eventually, the room service lady threatened us with her squeegee if we didn't leave immediately.

"Sorry," I said, turning around to face her. "We were just—"

I stopped cold. Someone had been watching us. I'd only caught a glimpse of his or her head as it disappeared around the corner of the hallway.

"Come on, Milly!" I yelled. "I think I just saw Marco!"

The two of us took off in hot pursuit. As we blew past the maid's cart, I grabbed a toilet brush to corner Marco with. (An old trick I'd learned from my mother.) We dashed around the corner, just in time to see the elevator door close with a *ding*.

"Crap!" I mashed the button like a cocaine-addicted rat in a lab experiment. No luck. "Come on. Let's take the stairs!"

Milly hobbled behind me in her designer sandals while I scurried down one and a half flights of stairs before tripping on my cheap flip-flops. I tumbled the rest of the way down and crashed into the wall.

"Oh, no, Val!" Milly cried out. "Are you okay?" She hobbled down the stairs to where I lay in the stairwell. The horrified look on her face didn't bode well.

"What?" I asked. "Am I bleeding?" Fearing the worst, I swished my tongue around my teeth. All present and accounted for, thank goodness.

"No." Milly's face puckered with disgust "That toilet wand. It must've broken. The brush part is ... *stuck in your hair.*"

I cringed. "Gross! Get it out, Milly! Get it out!"

Milly shook her head. "I love you, but no."

"Eeew!" I squealed as I reached up, felt around for the brush, then yanked it out of my tangled tresses. I flung it to the floor and scrambled to my feet. "Come on!"

We took off again. but the impromptu tumble down the stairs had cost me greatly in both dignity and time. As Milly and I burst through the stairway door and into the lobby, I caught a fleeting glimpse of a man in a Hawaiian shirt as he slipped out the door. I chased after him, waving the sharp end of my broken toilet brush over my head like the Ty D Bol woman gone mad.

I raced through the lobby. But once I blew through the doors to the outside, I stopped in my tracks. Everywhere I looked were guys in Hawaiian shirts. The place was swarming with them!

"Is there some kind of luau going on I don't know about?" I asked Milly. She didn't answer. I turned around to find she wasn't there. "Milly?"

I took a step back toward the lobby. Suddenly, my path was blocked by a man in a sharp, gray business suit.

"I'm sorry," he said. "But we must ask that you leave the premises immediately."

I blanched. "What? Why? What have *I* done?"

I took another step toward the lobby. Through the glass doors I spotted Milly staring back at me like a deer caught in the headlights of a Mack truck.

"What?" I mouthed to her.

Milly nodded to her left. I followed her gaze. In a huge mirror, I caught the reflection of some crazy, red-faced woman with a Phyllis Diller hairdo and green lips, brandishing a broken toilet wand.

My shoulders slumped. I looked up at the guy in the suit and said, "I'll see myself out."

• • • •

"WHY DIDN'T YOU STICK up for me in there?" I asked Milly after she slank out of the lobby a couple of minutes later.

Her eyes darted left and right, then she whispered, "You got banned from the lobby, Val. If we're going to find Marco, one of us needs to be able to still get back inside the hotel."

I sighed. "Fair point. Crap. What are we going to do now?"

Milly's eyes lit up. "I know! I'll go ask Thonii at reception for the room number for that attorney you were talking about. Bardsmore, right?"

"For fifty bucks?" I scoffed. "No way. If Thonii wants another Grant, he can go apply for one at the university. As far as I'm concerned, we're fresh out of Grant money."

"Then what'll we do?"

I ditched the toilet wand in the bushes and ran my fingers through my bedraggled hair. After thinking about it, I instantly regretted my decision. But there was no turning back now.

"Come on," I said. "Let's go back to the pool. That McLester guy was supposed to be keeping an eye out for Marco. As disgusting as he may be, I need to talk to him."

"Fine," Milly said. "But Val, fix your lipstick first. Your frog lips are showing."

• • • •

MILLIE AND I PICKED our way between lounge chairs and up to the tiki bar. After my botched investigation and a tumble down the stairs, I was in desperate need of that blue daiquiri we'd left behind with Jeri. But the place was still swarming with men in Hawaiian shirts.

143

"How are we gonna find McLester in this crowd?" Milly asked.

"Thelma!" a man called out. "Louise!"

I grabbed Milly's arm. "That's *him*, Milly."

"Who?"

"McLester. Now listen carefully. I'm Thelma. You're Louise. I lied to him about our names yesterday."

Milly pursed her lips and shook her head. "Of course you did, Ms. Green Tongue."

I rolled my eyes, then turned to face McLester and his disconcerting belly.

"Thelma!" McLester called out again. He was making a beeline for me, his arms open wide and his Hawaiian shirt open wider. To my horror, his entire body from head to toe appeared to be oozing sweat.

I slapped on a fake smile, then took up position behind a lounge chair so he couldn't slime me.

"You never called," he said. "I'm still waiting to take you ladies out."

"That's nice," I said. "Listen, have you seen Marco since he stiffed you yesterday?"

McLester grinned lasciviously. "No. But I wouldn't mind being stiffed by *you two*."

Milly leaned in and whispered in my ear. "Make this quick. I'm going to the restroom to throw up."

I whispered back. "I'll be right behind you."

• • • •

AFTER MAKING MY ESCAPE from McLester, Milly and I made a mad dash from the ladies' room back to the parking lot.

Once I caught my breath enough to be able to speak again, I told Milly what I'd gleaned from talking to McLester.

"He hasn't seen Marco either. But he said he'll call us if he sees him again."

Milly's face twisted in horror. "Don't tell me you gave that guy your phone number!"

I smirked. "No. I gave him yours."

Milly's eyes doubled in size. "You *what*?"

I laughed. "I'm just kidding. I gave him the number for Belated Rooms."

Milly scowled. "Gee whiz, Val. Don't ever scare me like that again!"

"I won't. I promi—"

Suddenly my face went slack. I'd just spotted something that made me freeze in my tracks.

It wasn't a ghost.

It wasn't a goblin.

It was a *Gremlin*.

Chapter Thirty

"**F**inkerman!" I yelled across the parking lot of the Don Cesar. I'd just spotted his ugly orange Gremlin in the lot. The slimeball attorney had to be lurking around somewhere nearby. "Finkerman, where are you?"

A patch of fuzzy red hair poked up above the top of a silver Mercedes two cars away.

"What are *you* doing here?" I hissed.

The rest of his head rose from behind the Mercedes. "Uh ... just keeping an eye out for you. You know, kind of like your bodyguard."

I sneered. "Yeah, right. You don't care about me. You just want to make sure I don't skip town, so you don't lose out on your cut of a million dollars."

"What are you two talking about?" Milly asked.

I cringed. In the heat of the moment, I'd forgotten Milly didn't know anything about the murder charges or my deal with Finkerman to sue Marco Shamway.

Crap! I had to make sure Finkerman wouldn't spill the beans on me! Finkerman sprinted toward me. His mouth began to open. I waved my hands wildly, trying to stop him from speaking. But it was too late. That tomcat was already clawing its way out of the bag.

"Didn't she tell you?" Finkerman said to Milly. "We're suing Marco Shamway for her cut of the Hunk Clock." He winked and patted me on the back. "Right after we get her off the hook for murder, of course."

• • • •

"AND THAT'S THE WHOLE story in a nutshell," I said to Milly as she, Finkerman, and I sat in the air-conditioned comfort of her luxurious red Beemer.

"Oh, Val," Milly said. "Why does this stuff always happen to you? It's unbelievable."

"I know, right?" Finkerman said. He scooted up in the backseat, causing his knobby knees to poke up to his shoulders like a giant grasshopper. "Just sitting here this extra fifteen minutes is gonna cost me over twenty bucks more for parking!"

I turned and shot Finkerman a sour look. "Glad to see you have your priorities in order."

He jabbed my shoulder with a boney finger. "Just so you know, Fremden, this parking fee is going on my expense account."

I swatted his finger away. "Fine. Take it out of your cut of the million dollars."

Finkerman stared at me for a second, then laughed.

I frowned. "What's so funny?"

He smirked. "I just noticed your tongue. What's the matter, Fremden? Feeling kinda *Blustered?*"

I sneered. "Yeah. Thanks to *you!*"

"Poor Val," Milly said. "There ought to be a law against those horrible Blusters!"

Finkerman's thin lips puckered to one side. "Now that you mention it, I just read something about Blusters in this morning's *Jail Bait Journal.*"

My nose crinkled. "*Jail Bait what?*"

"The *Jail Bait Journal,*" Finkerman said. "It's the online magazine for lawyers on the go."

Milly cocked her blonde head. "Lawyers on the go?"

I rolled my eyes. "He means on the lam—or living in their cars."

"I mean no such thing," Finkerman huffed. "Check your privilege, Fremden."

"Fine. Now *tell us what's going on with the Circle-J Blusters before I throttle you!*"

Finkerman leaned back in the seat, putting distance between us. "Well, according to a recent release by the FDA,

kiwi flavored Blusters contain some sort of toxic green dye.
And perhaps just a smidgen of formaldehyde."

"Argh!" I groaned. "We should sue them!"

Finkerman tapped a boney finger on his temple. "Already
on it. Hey, stick out your tongue, Fremden."

I scowled. "What for?"

"So I can take a picture. For *evidence*. I'm gonna file a
civil suit against Circle-J. Hold on. Is there anything left of
that Bluster you bought?"

"No. I drank it all."

Finkerman sighed. "Too bad." Suddenly, he perked up
again. "Wait. If you still have the cup, I could lick it."

My upper lip snarled. "You'd poison yourself for money?
That's pathetic."

Finkerman shrugged. "Well, unlike you, the only person
who might die from *my* actions would be *me*."

I closed my eyes and shook my head.

*What am I doing arguing with this idiot about some
stupid convenience-store slushie when my life is at stake?*

I took a deep breath and tried to focus. "Moving on,
everyone. Finkerman, were you able to reach Anthony
Bardsmore last night?"

Finkerman shook his head. "No. But I left a message on
his phone."

"Oh!" Milly said. "You mean the guy in the red Ferrari?"

I nodded. "Yeah. That reminds me. Finkerman, we saw
his car leaving the parking lot when we were coming in
today. He might be staying at the Don Cesar."

"Interesting." Finkerman glanced around the parking lot.
"Or Bardsmore could be working with a guest at the hotel.
Namely, *Marco Shamway*."

I chewed my lip. "I thought about that, too. Could you try
calling him again?"

"No can do, Muchacha. I don't make phone calls from
cars."

"But you're in the back seat!" I said.

"Still, it's against my principles."

I scowled. "What principles?"

"The principle that it costs a dollar and a half a minute to park in this ridiculous lot!" Finkerman said. "Look, I think we're done here for the time being. I'm leaving while I can still afford to pay the tab."

"Fine."

Finkerman opened the back door. "I'll call Bardsmore as soon as I find a place to pull over."

"Thanks," I said as he slammed the back door.

Through the windshield, Milly and I watched the low-rent lawyer sprint over to his Gremlin, then peel out toward the parking booth.

Milly cranked the engine on her Beemer. "You know what they say about a man who drives a red Ferrari?"

I smirked. "That he's 'compensating' for something?"

Milly nodded. "Exactly. But what does it say about a man when he drives a rusted-out Gremlin?"

"My guess? That he hasn't been 'compensated' since the Carter administration."

Chapter Thirty-One

M illy and I were cruising down Gulf Boulevard looking for a place to have lunch when my cell phone buzzed. It was Finkerman.

"I was right!" he shouted into my ear. "Bardsmore wants to meet about a proposal to offer you a 10% royalty share in the Hunk Clock profits!"

I nearly swallowed my tonsils. "Are you serious?"

"So serious that lunch is on me."

I nearly dropped the phone. With Finkerman, it didn't get any more serious than that.

"Meet me at the Perky Pelican," he said.

"You got it." I clicked off the phone and grinned from ear to ear. For a shot at *that* kind of money, I'd have met Finkerman under the Gandy Bridge.

• • • •

"ARE YOU REALLY GOING to get a 10% share in the Hunk Clock?" Milly asked, peering out from behind her menu. She reached across the table and grabbed my arm. "That's fabulous!"

"What kind of money are we talking about?" I asked Finkerman.

"Hmm." His eyes darted left to right as he looked up at the ceiling. "Potentially? I'd say over a million bucks."

"So I don't have to sue him for it," I said. "Think of it, Milly. I could be a millionaire!"

"Oh, Val!" Milly said. "I'm so glad for you!"

"Ahem," Finkerman said, clearing his throat. "That's a million *minus* my 40% legal representation fees, of course."

My eyes narrowed. "I'll pay you 20%, Finkerman. Not a dime more."

"But—"

I didn't let him finish. "Take the deal or I'm hiring somebody else."

Finkerman frowned. "Like who?"

I arched an eyebrow. "Like, pretty much *anybody* else on the planet."

"Ugh." Finkerman raised his menu to cover his face. "Fine. I'll just have to get Bardsmore to increase your royalty percentage."

I nearly blanched. "You can do that?"

"Of course."

"Cool! Wait a minute. First you have to get me cleared of murder charges. Otherwise, this whole million dollars is a moot point. I mean, I can't exactly spend all that cash if I'm locked up in jail for life, now can I?"

Finkerman peeked over his menu at me and grinned. "No. But on the bright side, *I* still can!"

• • • •

WITH A MEETING SET up between Finkerman and Bardsmore for tomorrow morning, I returned to Belated Rooms with a spring in my step. In the not-to-distant future, I was going to be a millionaire! What's more, Geraldine would be back in a day or two as well. Soon, my whole stint as a flat-broke junk-store flunkie would be over.

Oh, yeah! No more second-hand life for me!

I rubbed my hands together with glee. What would I do with my fortune? First off, when Tom came back from his special assignment, I was going to buy him a red Ferrari! Not that the man had any shortcomings he needed to compensate for ...

I smiled at the thought of surprising Tom. Then I smiled even bigger at the thought of kissing him. Suddenly, like a pinprick to a balloon, my daydream blew apart. I remembered that woman giggling on the recorder. The tinkle of her laughter echoed in my brain.

Stop it, Val. Can't you just enjoy the moment?

Apparently not. I set my purse down on the counter next to the cash register, closed my eyes, and took a deep breath.

This is all going to work out just fine.

My cell phone buzzed, startling me. I fished around amongst the crumpled heap of receipts in my purse and pulled out my phone. "Hello?"

"Val Fremden?"

"Uh ... who wants to know?"

"This is Sergeant McNulty."

"Oh. Hello, sir."

"Do you know a man named Marco Shamway?

"Yeah. Why?"

"According to one of my officers, several people overheard you talking with a blonde woman yesterday about wanting to kill him."

I winced. "Oh. About that. Look. The guy's a jerk. I mean, he treated me badly in high school. And he stole my idea and made a fortune with it. But I just found out—"

"I see," McNulty said. "Thank you."

"Thanks?" I asked. "For what?"

"Supplying the motive. As it turns out, the dead man in the box is Marco Shamway. But I suppose you already knew that."

Chapter Thirty-Two

N*o no no no no no no!*

How could my future have gone from millionaire to murderer in one phone call flat?

I slumped against the checkout counter. Sergeant McNulty had given me one hour to report to the police station on my own steam before he sent an officer over to collect me. Marco Shamway was dead, and I'd gone and blabbed all over town about wanting to kill the jerk.

Could this possibly get any worse?

I chewed my bottom lip and wondered what other incriminating evidence McNulty might have against me. He said he had more questions for me. What kind of questions could he have? Would he let me go afterward? Or was this the last time I'd ever see the light of day?

I shoved my phone back into my purse and glanced around at the filthy junkpile that was Belated Rooms. Would this crap-hole be the last thing I ever laid eyes on as a free woman?

• • • •

WITH A DEATH GRIP ON the steering wheel and Tom Petty blaring on the radio, I wracked my brain, trying to figure out how to prove my innocence to McNulty.

Marco Shamway was dead, and I was his prime suspect!

Distracted by the thought of having to share a cell and a stainless-steel toilet with a woman named Chuck for the next 30 years, I nearly rear-ended someone at a red light. I stomped the brakes just in time to keep from colliding into the backend of a shiny new Tesla.

Get ahold of yourself! You're innocent. You have nothing to worry about!

Then why am I biting my fingernails to the quick? I spit the remains of a gnawed nail out the window. Then I shook my head at my sorry state, and the homegrown stupidity that had landed me in it.

Pulverizing figurines? Seriously? Why in the world did I have to pick such an idiotic habit? Why couldn't I have ... I dunno ... been a compulsive cleaner, like Tom? Then all I could be accused of is scrubbing the finish off something!

The light turned green. I punched the gas pedal, keeping my distance from the Tesla. Deep down inside, I knew my life's problems couldn't be solved with a hammer. But smashing things to smithereens was my Prozac.

Over the years, my Hammer of Justice had helped me cope with some particularly bad life choices. How was I supposed to know that cavorting with my beloved HOJ would end up being my ruination?

Even now, as my Hammer of Justice was about to cost me my freedom, I wasn't sure I could give it up. The healing force of smashing things to bits ran so deep within me, it was practically in my DNA! Sure, it was a weird habit. But that didn't make me guilty of murder.

It had all been a stupid, knee-jerk accident!

I had to convince McNulty of that—and that someone else was to blame. It was simple. Someone had broken into my garage and stolen my Hammer of Justice. Then they'd killed my mortal enemy Marco with it and dumped his body off in the alley behind where I worked—stuffed inside one of my friend J.D.'s moving boxes that I'd helped transport there ...

My shoulders drooped.

Oh, geez. This does not *look good.*

Who would believe all that? More to the point, who would actually do *all of that? Only someone who had it out for me, big time. But who?*

I pulled into the police station parking lot and cut the engine. I sat and lingered inside Shabby Maggie for a few minutes, contemplating my fate. As I stared up at the sky, raindrops began to pelt the windshield like tears.

I swallowed hard, climbed out of the car, and shuffled toward the police station in the rain.

Please, universe. Please don't let this be the last free breath I ever take.

Chapter Thirty-Three

"**W**hat happened to your mouth?" Sergeant McNulty asked as he sat down across the table from me in the interrogation room.

My hair and clothes damp from getting caught in the rain shower, I slumped in my chair like a wet dishrag. "If you must know, I was attacked by a poisonous kiwi Bluster, okay? That hardly seems like a relevant question."

"I wouldn't be too certain about that."

I eyed McNulty. "What do you mean?"

"It's looking more like Marco Shamway wasn't beaten to death, but *poisoned*."

"Poisoned?" I sat up in my chair. "Then that would prove I'm innocent!"

"Unless you poisoned him."

My mouth fell open. "Are you serious?"

"I find it interesting that you would mention being poisoned when it appears that Shamway was. Are you trying to cover your tracks? Did you ingest a non-lethal dose yourself, so you could pretend to be just another victim?"

"No! That's ridiculous!"

McNulty studied me. "Is it? Tell me. Do you have access to poisons in your line of work?"

"At the thrift shop?" I grimaced. "Not unless you want to gnaw the lead paint off the windowsills."

McNulty's eyes narrowed. "So, you've thought about it."

I blanched. "What?"

"I'm going to need a detailed timeline of your every move for the last 72 hours."

"Everything?" I asked.

Even when I took a poop?

"Yes. You don't have anything to hide, do you?"

Well, yeah. This morning, that stupid Bluster had gone through me like grease through a goose. I almost didn't make it to the bathroom in time. Did I have to write that in my report? Ugh. Maybe it didn't matter. With any luck, the Bluster's toxic green goo would kick in soon and I'd never make it to trial.

Come on, Bluster ...

• • • •

IT SEEMED LIKE A MILLION years had passed since I'd bopped Melvin Flemster in the head with a pizza pan, but that was where my 72-hour timeline for McNulty began. It ended with me staring at the sergeant from across the interrogation table, wondering if he was going to escort me out wearing those shiny silver handcuffs dangling from his belt.

McNulty glanced down at the timeline I'd scrawled on a notepad. "So, after you got fired from Tiffany's Temp Agency on Thursday, you say you went home and smashed a figurine of your ex-employer, Melvin Flemster."

Not exactly. That day Laverne had caught me pounding a figurine in the garage, I'd actually been exorcizing my pent-up rage at Marco. But what difference did it make?

I nodded. "More or less."

McNulty shook his head. "You've got some real issues, Fremden."

"Thanks."

"After that, you assisted your neighbor Laverne Cowens in disposing of four boxes of goods stolen from her husband."

"Yes. But they weren't exactly *stolen goods*."

"Perhaps. But you *did* steal a figurine from Belated Rooms, didn't you? You were caught by the proprietor, Geraldine Jiggles. In exchange for leniency, you agreed to work in her shop over the weekend."

"If that's what you're calling blackmail nowadays, then yes, that's correct."

McNulty pursed his lips. "After your unpaid training day, on the drive home you discovered the billboard with Marco Shamway and his Hunk Clock."

"No. That's not right. I spotted the billboard earlier that morning, right after I got fired from Tiffany's Temps."

McNulty shot me an *I got you* look. "So, the figurine you claim you smashed of Flemster could've actually been of Marco Shamway."

Man this guy doesn't miss a thing!

My nose crinkled. "Does it matter?"

"Absolutely." McNulty stared me down. "If you practiced killing Shamway prior to his death, it could prove intent, and that's first-degree premeditation."

"But I didn't kill Marco!"

"Right." McNulty glanced down at the notebook. "It says here that the next day, you recruited your friend Milly Halbert to help you track down Shamway."

"Yes."

"What exactly did you plan on doing when you found him?"

I shrugged. "I dunno. Cuss him out?"

"That hardly seems like a satisfying punishment for a man who supposedly stole your idea and the fortune that was due you from it."

I scowled. "What else *could* I have done? I don't have any proof the idea was mine. Besides, Milly and I weren't able to find him."

"But you *did* find him, Fremden. Dead in the alley behind your workplace, Belated Rooms."

I gulped, feeling like a rat in a trap. "Well, yeah. But I didn't know it was him. Geez! I'd only been working at that stupid place for one day!"

McNulty's dark eyes narrowed. "Which in my book makes the chance of this all being a coincidence even *more* remote, not less."

I sat up and tried to gather my thoughts, along with some backbone. "Look, Sergeant McNulty. First you accused me of killing Marco with a hammer. That wasn't true. Then you said I killed him with my Hammer of Justice. That wasn't true either. Now you're saying I poisoned him? What next? Will you accuse me of shooting him with a bow and arrow?"

"Do you *own* a bow and arrow, Ms. Fremden?"

"No!"

McNulty glanced down at the timeline I'd written. "You say here that you and your friend Milly went to the Don Cesar, then you returned to work. That's when you discovered Marco Shamway in the box."

"Yes."

McNulty shot me a stern look. "Clever, setting up an alibi with Ms. Halbert."

I frowned. "What are you talking about?"

"You couldn't move Shamway's body by yourself. You recruited your best friend to help you. The two of you dumped Shamway in the alley behind the shop, then took off to the Don Cesar to create an alibi."

My temper flared. "Are you kidding? Leave Milly out of this. She isn't capable of hurting a fly. She'd never have helped me move a dead body. She didn't even want to go inside Belated Rooms for fear she might catch something."

McNulty locked eyes with me. "Then who helped you?"

"What?" I yelled. "Nobody! Look, I'm telling the truth. For all I know, Marco was already in the alley before I even got to Belated Rooms yesterday. I never went out there until after Milly dropped me off after we went to the Don Cesar."

"Can you prove that?"

"No. I mean, who could? I didn't go to the alley yesterday morning because there was no need for me to. The only reason I went out there yesterday afternoon was to dump the boxes I'd broken down in the storeroom. It's part of my job."

"Right."

"Besides, why would I kill Marco when he's going to give me 10% of the profits from the Hunk Clock?"

McNulty's eyes lit up. "So, there's money involved." He smiled cruelly. "There's always money involved."

"No!" I said. "I mean yes, there's money. But I only found out about it today."

"How is that possible, when Marco Shamway was dead?"

"I heard from his attorney," I explained, nervously wringing my hands. "Well, I mean *my* attorney heard it from *his* attorney. They're meeting tomorrow to hash out the contract."

"Let me guess. You're asking for more money?"

I winced. "Maybe. So what?"

"Greed is also a common reason for homicide."

Oh, crap. Maybe I shouldn't have pushed Finkerman. Then again ...

"Hold on, Sergeant McNulty. I'm already getting money from Marco. Why would I kill the golden goose?"

He raised an eyebrow. "You said you just found out about the money today. Perhaps you killed the goose before you knew it was golden."

I shook my head. "I can't win with you, can I?"

"No. So stop trying."

"I will as soon as you stop trying to book me for murder!" I slumped in my chair. "Can't you at least *entertain* the idea that what I'm telling you is the truth?"

"Fair enough," McNulty said, setting the notebook aside on the table. "Where is this so-called meeting between attorneys taking place?"

"At the Don Cesar."

"Do you plan on attending?"

"No. I mean ... I kind of can't."

"Why not?"

I gritted my teeth. There were a number of reasons, the biggest being that I'd been asked to leave the place and never come back ...

"It's a lawyer-to-lawyer thing," I said. "Plus, I have to work at Belated Rooms."

McNulty shot me a *yeah, right* look. "You'd miss a shot at increasing your fortune just to earn a measly paycheck at that disgusting thrift shop?"

I shrugged. "What can I say? I'm a dedicated employee."

McNulty laughed. "Now I know for sure."

"Know what?"

"That you're a liar."

"I am not!" I bellowed. "Well, not about killing Marco, anyway. How did you figure out the guy in the box was him, anyway?"

"You already know how. You ditched his wallet in the dumpster along with your other hammer. Not the brightest move on your part."

"But I didn't touch his wallet! And you said Marco wasn't killed with a hammer!"

"Maybe not," McNulty said. "But finding Shamway's wallet and your Hammer of Justice links you to the crime scene, Fremden. The likelihood of someone stealing your hammer from your garage and then killing your sworn enemy with it are about as likely as me drinking a kiwi Bluster and going to the moon. Not impossible, but highly improbable."

"I'm telling the truth about not killing him," I said. "I swear! How can I prove it to you?"

"Not by telling me you didn't do it over and over again." McNulty frowned. "Unfortunately, both hammers and the wallet had been wiped clean of prints. Otherwise, I'd lock you up right now."

The air went out of me. I slumped in my chair.

"Oh, cheer up, Ms. Fremden. The way it's looking for you right now, the worst is yet to come."

161

Chapter Thirty-Four

As I followed McNulty through the maze of locked metal doors and dim corridors that led from the prison-like interrogation room back toward the escape hatch of the lobby, I wracked my brain. I *had* to think of a way to clear my name so that I never had to set foot in this place again.

I hadn't killed Marco. So, who else could it be? The only person I could think of who even *knew* Marco was Milly. But Marco was already in that box in the alley before either of us even knew he was in town. Plus, she'd never do anything like that.

Who in the world could have killed Marco?

As Sergeant McNulty opened the last locked door between me and the lobby, I suddenly thought of another name.

"You're free to go for now," McNulty said. "But like I said before. Don't leave town."

I gasped. "Wait a minute! What if Marco's attorney killed him?"

McNulty's eyes narrowed. "Why would the man's attorney want to kill him?"

"You obviously never met Marco when he was alive." As soon as the words left my lips, I realized that I'd shot myself in the foot—again.

McNulty studied me with those dark eyes of his. "No, I haven't. But *you* have."

I grimaced. "Well, yes. But I haven't seen him in like 30 years. Back in high school Marco was a jerk. But that's not the point I meant to make."

"Then what is?"

"I *meant* to say that attorneys can be cheating lowlifes, too. I've been ripped off by lawyers more times than I care to remember."

"I'm still waiting for your point?"

"I thought I just made it."

McNulty crossed his arms. "Are you implying that I'm dense?"

I groaned inside. Why did I have to be born with impatience as my superpower?

"I'm sorry," I backpedaled. "Let me start over. You see, it's been my experience that whoever handles the legal paperwork usually ends up with the lion's share of the loot."

"I've seen it happen," McNulty agreed. "So?"

"So, maybe Marco's attorney thought that with his client dead, he'd be free to alter the paperwork. You know. And claim the Hunk Clock fortune for himself."

McNulty studied me. "It's a lead, Fremden. Not a great one. But a lead nevertheless." He uncrossed his arms. "As a public servant, I'm bound to do my due diligence with it. Okay, what's Shamway's attorney's name?"

"Anthony Bardsmore. I don't have his card. I gave it to Finkerman. But I can call him and get it." I started to rummage through my purse for my phone. McNulty stopped me.

"No," he said. "Don't call him."

"Why not?"

"You said Finkerman's meeting with Bardsmore tomorrow morning at the Don Cesar."

"Yes."

"What time?"

"Eleven o'clock. Why?"

McNulty's brow furrowed. "I think it might be worth going there as a fly on the wall. To see if either of them says anything incriminating."

My heart skipped a beat. Was McNulty changing his tune about me? "Really?" I asked. "That's great! I'll go with you!"

McNulty grimaced. "No!"

"Why not? I could help—"

"Finkerman would recognize you. That would blow my cover."

"Oh. Right. But how will *you* recognize *them*?"

McNulty shot me a dubious look. "I've met Finkerman, remember? And as they say, some things you just can't unsee."

I blew out a sigh. "True enough."

• • • •

I WOKE UP THE NEXT morning to my phone buzzing. McNulty was on the end of the line.

"Just a reminder call," he said. "Don't get any bright ideas today."

"Bright ideas?" I asked.

At this time in the morning? Without coffee? Not a chance.

"What I mean is, I don't want to see you at the Don Cesar today. Got it?"

I sat up in bed. "Yes, sir. No problem."

"It better not be. I'm telling you, Ms. Fremden. if I see you there, I'll arrest you for interfering with an investigation."

"Fine. I said I wouldn't go."

"It could be dangerous."

"Dangerous?" I asked. "Why would you think going to a meeting between Finkerman and Bardsmore could be *dangerous*?"

"Because there's definitely something fishy going on with Anthony Bardsmore."

"Fishy?"

"Yes. Let's just say he's not a stranger to the police up in North Dakota."

I blanched. "Oh, my word! Has he killed before? Are you going to arrest him on outstanding warrants or something?"

"No," McNulty said. "That would be rather difficult to do, considering Anthony Bardsmore died 15 years ago."

Chapter Thirty-Five

My hands shook as I held the bottle of spray disinfectant. I aimed it at the filthy front door of Belated Rooms, but missed and hit the sidewalk. Like a heroin addict on Methadone, I had a major case of the DT's. But in my case, I was trying to replace my figurine-smashing habit with my boyfriend Tom's penchant for cleaning things to within an inch of their lives.

It wasn't working.

I shot a nervous glance through the window at the clock on the wall. I'd begun my killer cleaning spree at 10 a.m. It was now 10:03, and I was jonesing to smash a figurine so badly I could taste porcelain on the tip of my still slightly green tongue.

How am I supposed to just sit around and wait for McNulty to call me after Finkerman's meeting with Bardsmore?

I chewed my bottom lip. My whole life was in the hands of McNulty and Finkerman. The first one had it out for me. The second one ... well, had it out for me, too!

I glanced at the clock again. It was 10:04.

I'm never gonna make it to noon.

I gave up cleaning the door and went back inside. Besides committing hari-kari, losing consciousness was my only chance of surviving until McNulty called.

I walked over to the furniture corner. After careful consideration of the disgusting options, I curled up on the least offensive old couch in the jumbled showroom. But, of course, I couldn't sleep. Hell. I couldn't even close my eyes!

What should I do, universe? Please. Send me a sign!

As if on cue, the front door to the thrift shop croaked like a love-crazed toad. I bolted up off the couch. A skinny old woman in a sparkling gold lamé jumpsuit waved at me.

"Hi, Laverne."

"Hey, Val!" She grinned at me, then her smile faded. "Are you okay?"

"Huh? Oh, sure." I shot her my best fake smile. "Are you two love birds all moved in?"

"Snug as two bugs in a rug, Honey. After the condo committee found out I wasn't a stripper, it was all smooth sailing, thanks to J.D.'s testimony."

"Uh ... that's great, Laverne. So, what are you doing *here*?"

"Well, J.D.'s birthday is coming up." Laverne smiled sheepishly. "I was wondering if you had any of those Hummels left?"

I cringed. "Uh ... no. Sorry."

"Darn."

"But I bet you could find some at the antique store a few doors down. That guy Eber bought them all."

"Every single one?"

"Yeah."

Then I remembered there was one exception. I still had that Happy Traveler figurine I'd sort of shoplifted from Geraldine. I'd stashed it under a pile of junk beneath the cash register so I wouldn't smash it. A kind of "break in case of emergency" move.

Geez. Maybe I really am *a junkie.*

"Hold on, Laverne." I ducked under the register and pulled Happy Traveler from his garbage-filled dungeon. "I just remembered. I saved this one."

I set it on the counter. Laverne's eyes lit up.

"Oh, that's perfect, Val! What do I owe you?"

"Nothing. It's on the house."

Laverne appeared confused. "But this isn't your house, Val."

"Oh. That's true. But I kind of negotiated this little guy into my deal for helping out Geraldine. It's mine. Take it as my gift to you."

Laverne pouted. "But I need a gift *for J.D.*"

I stifled a smirk. "Okay, then. It's my gift to J.D."

Laverne winced. "But what would *I* give him then?"

"I know," I said. "How about let's make it a gift from both of us."

The clouds lifted from Laverne's face. She beamed at me. "Perfect! Oh, you're a lifesaver, Val!"

"Not really."

Laverne picked up the figurine. "Well, I can't say he's cute. But at least he's small."

I laughed, then remembered how I'd gotten the figurine in the first place. "Uh, Laverne? You might want to wash that thing. You never know where it's been."

"Will do." Laverne gushed over the Happy Traveler, then glanced up at me. Her smile faded. "Why so glum, Honey?"

I shrugged. "It's nothing."

Just my life is going down the toilet as we speak, and I can't do a damn thing about it.

"You look itchy," Laverne said.

She was right. Every molecule in my body wanted to bolt out the door and drive like a maniac to the Don Cesar.

I desperately wanted to be a second fly on the wall along with McNulty. But he'd threatened to charge me with tampering with his investigation if I showed my face there—not to mention that guy in the suit who'd banned me from the lobby. I blew out a sigh.

Laverne wrapped a long, skinny arm around my shoulder. "Aww. Cheer up, Honey. Is there anything I can do?"

"Not really." Then a thought struck me. "You know what, Laverne? I think I have an idea."

I never said it was a *good* one.

• • • •

I STUDIED MY REFLECTION through the cracks in the full-length mirror. I was trying to see what my butt looked like, but it was obscured by the duct-tape price tag stuck in the center of the glass. I took a step closer to the mirror and reached for the tape.

Geraldine wants $3.75 for this piece of crap? Is she crazy?

"You look fabulous, Val!" Laverne said.

I glanced up at my neighbor. She was grinning proudly, hands clasped, like a mother admiring her bridezilla-to-be.

I chewed my bottom lip. I didn't share her confidence.

When it came to playing dress-up, Laverne Cowens had her own unique style. I mean, the woman was wearing a gold lamé jumpsuit, for crying out loud! But I was desperate. So desperate that a birdbrain in the hand had seemed worth two in the bush.

"You don't think this red wig looks trashy?" I asked.

Laverne shook her head. "Not at all! Especially with that flashy diamond comb tucked in the side. You look like Ginger on *Gilligan's Island*!"

Only if she never got rescued—and then ate the rest of the crew.

"I dunno, Laverne. I want to blend in, not make a ... um ... *fashion statement*. I just want to disguise myself so McNulty and Finkerman don't recognize me."

"Hmm." Laverne studied me for a moment. "I know! You need a fake mole on your upper lip. That would be the perfect touch!"

I crinkled my nose. "Only if I'm trying to win best lookalike for Marilyn Monroe's grandmother."

"Pish-posh." Laverne patted my puffed-sleeve shoulder. "Besides, with the cleavage you're showing in that tight purple dress, nobody's gonna be looking at your *face* anyways."

"Are you sure?" I glanced at my rear again. "My butt looks like two bowling balls trying to wrestle their way out of Prince's gym bag."

"Tiddlywinks!" Laverne said. "You look great! Hey, what time is that meeting you've got to go to?"

"Eleven."

Laverne grinned. "Oh, good. You've still got twenty-two minutes to make it!"

Chapter Thirty-Six

W*hat the hell am I doing?*

I'd just left a crazy old lady in charge of Belated Rooms, and now I was hurtling down Gulf Boulevard toward a date with certain disaster—fashion-wise at the bare minimum. If I didn't pop a dress seam before I got to the Don Cesar, McNulty would surely pop a cap in my ass if he saw through my disguise.

I pressed a stiletto-clad foot down on the gas pedal. But as anyone who's ever been in a hurry knows, desperation breeds red traffic lights. I hit every single one along the way—including the light at the intersection where Marco's annoying billboard stood.

Riddled with anxiety, adrenaline, and idiocy, I glared up at Marco's oversized effigy and drummed my nails on the steering wheel, hoping Laverne's tarantula-thick mascara job wouldn't melt into raccoon eyes before I got to the restaurant.

Ugh. There he is. Marco Shamway—still mocking me from the grave in all his perfect, sexy glory. Meanwhile, here I sit looking like the loser of a drag queen bingo tournament.

Even though I now knew Marco planned to give me 10% of his fortune, I still resented the jerk. After all, the idea for the Hunk Clock was mine. That was worth at least 50% of the royalties, *right*?

My fingers squeezed the steering wheel like ten stubby anacondas as I thought back to my pathetic teenage self.

Who could I have become in life if Marco hadn't tortured away what little self-esteem I'd had back then? What better life choices would I have made if I'd had the luxury of a comfy fortune to fall back on?

Sure, I might not have become president of the United States. But if I had money, I certainly wouldn't be headed for a sketchy stakeout in a skanky red wig and a cheap prom dress two sizes too small, now would I?

I scowled at the blasted billboard and the man who had ruined my life.

What justice is there for people like me?

Then I spotted it. A little bit of justice.

Someone had drawn a moustache on Marco. A long, thin, curly-ended Snidely Whiplash moustache. And they'd blacked out one of his front teeth.

I smirked like Cruella Deville.

Maybe there was a caring Creator out there after all ...

• • • •

WHEN I PULLED UP TO the parking booth at the Don Cesar, the snotty little parking attendant didn't recognize me. He complimented my old Ford Falcon, then snuck a peek at my cleavage as I handed him one of the twenty-dollar bills I'd "borrowed" from the till at Belated Rooms.

Ha! I must not look so bad after all. But more importantly, my disguise is working. Ka-ching!

After parking Shabby Maggie in the shadiest spot I could find, I hobbled across the parking lot in my silver stilettos toward the restaurant. As I reached for the front door, I felt a seam pop on my dress.

Crap!

I surveyed the damage. Fortunately, the hole that had opened up was at my waist. I tucked my purse in the crook of my arm to hide it, then pushed open the door.

As I stepped inside the restaurant, the blast of cool air nearly knocked me over. The hot sweat drenching my armpits felt as if it had instantly turned to ice.

Ahhh!

I took a step toward the dining area. The waiter manning the entrance podium spotted me. His eyebrows rose an inch. Then he hurried over to me as quickly as his personal dignity would allow.

"Excuse me," he said in a hushed tone. "I believe there's been some mistake. Drag queen bingo isn't until *Saturday*."

Dang it. I knew it!

"Um ... I'm not here for—" I managed to say before I tripped on my thrift-store stilettos and fell into the waiter's arms.

He grunted from the impact. "Ma'am are you okay?"

"Uh ... yes. Just a little dizzy from the heat." I steadied myself on my feet and shot the waiter a weak smile. "Thank you for catching me!"

"Of course. Um ... how may I help you?"

"I—" I glanced over the waiter's shoulder and nearly fainted for real. Finkerman had emerged from the men's room and was headed right toward me.

Crap on a cracker!

Unable to think of anything better to do, I feigned a swoon and buried my face into the waiter's nice suit again.

"Oh, dear," the waiter said as Finkerman walked by. "Poor thing. That dress is so tight I bet you can't even breathe! Should I call someone? Do you need a doctor?"

"No, thank you." I gently pushed off him and steadied myself again on my stilettos. "I'll be okay. I just need to sit down for a minute. Maybe a sip of water, please?"

The impeccably dressed waiter tried not to look horrified at the prospect of me soiling his fine establishment. He tried, but failed.

"Um ... do you have a reservation?" he asked. "We're fully booked for lunch today."

"No. But I feel a little dizzy. I wouldn't want to fall and break my leg or something. That would be bad for both of us, wouldn't it? Could I just sit down for a minute or two?"

The waiter's petrified face softened a notch. "Okay. Come with me."

He took me by the arm and led me to a booth in a dark corner. It was marked with a placard that read *Reserved*. "You can sit here for a few minutes. I'll get you some water."

"Thank you so much!" I glanced around the restaurant and spotted what I was looking for. Finkerman's signature frizzy comb-over. It was poking up above the backrest of a booth two tables down.

"Oh my," I said, fanning my face with my hand. "The air conditioner is blowing on my head here. Do you mind?"

Before the waiter could object, I scrambled over to the empty booth directly behind Finkerman. It also had a *Reserved* placard. I plunked myself down on the bench facing away from Finkerman, so that we were sitting back-to-back.

I smiled triumphantly.

Ha! Phase one of my mission completed!

The waiter scurried up to the booth and hovered over me, a nervous look on his face. "Ma'am, I'm sorry but—"

"This is so much better," I said. "Thank you!"

"Well, I—"

I don't know what the waiter said after that. I never heard it. I was transfixed on the nasty brown stripe marring the collar of his crisp white shirt. I stifled a cringe, then smiled up at him demurely. "That glass of water, please?"

As I spoke, I felt something bounce off my upper lip. I glanced down. A small brown blob the size of an eraser tip was tumbling across the table like a rat turd.

My fake mole had fallen off.

I could tell by the look on the waiter's face that he'd seen it too. "Ma'am, I'm afraid—"

"Don't worry," I cooed, then flicked the fake mole off the table like a dried booger. "I'll scoot right on out of here as soon as the party with the reservation comes. I promise. All I need is a cold drink and a minute to catch my breath."

The waiter swallowed hard. His shoulders went limp. "As you wish."

• • • •

EVEN THOUGH I WAS SIPPING ice-cold water, I was growing hotter by the second.

173

The conversation going on between Finkerman and Bardsmore in the booth right behind me had me boiling mad. I fully expected that at any second, steam would blast out of both my ears like water from a whale's blowhole.

"Shamway's richer than God," I heard Bardsmore say. "Everywhere we go, people treat him like a celebrity. To be that loaded and good-looking ought to be a crime. And lemme tell you, you wouldn't *believe* all the hot chicks he gets."

"I know the feeling," Finkerman said.

I choked on a sip of water.

Seriously, Finkerman? The only hot chick you have a chance with comes with a side order of coleslaw and fries.

"I'd kill for a gig like yours," Finkerman said. "Private attorney to a millionaire? I bet you get a lot of his leftover side chicks."

"Not really," Bardsmore said. "It's just not fair. The only women attracted to me come with menu pricing, if you know what I mean. But at least *I'm* not the one selling my body for money. So, there's *that*."

"You know what the going rate is?" Finkerman asked.

"For a call girl?"

"No. For like, a gigolo gig."

Bardsmore laughed. "Nothing personal, but you and I are the kind of guys who *pay* for it—not *get* paid for it."

"Hmm. What about pimping, then?" Finkerman asked.

"Forget about it. You really want to manage a bunch of crazy-ass women? Besides, they're all going independent these days. And these gals are *everywhere*."

"Everywhere?"

"Yeah," Bardsmore said. "Too much competition these days. I'm telling you, the market is saturated. Hell, yesterday I even saw two prostitutes *here*. At the pool area."

Finkerman cleared his throat. "So, which way is the pool?"

"Don't bother," Bardsmore said. "The two I saw? Meh. The blonde wasn't that bad. But the brunette? Let's just say it's time that old war horse traded in her thong for a trip to the glue factory."

Finkerman laughed. "I just saw some redheaded hag fitting that description on my way back from the men's room. But I'm curious. You know, for research purposes."

"Curious about what?"

"How'd you know the pair at the pool were prostitutes?"

"Easy. They called themselves Thelma and Louise."

"You're kidding," Finkerman said. "How lame is that?"

"Well, actually it was pretty fitting," Bardsmore said. "Let me tell you, if I had to sleep with the brunette, I'd drive my car off a cliff, too."

The two men burst out laughing. My left eardrum popped. I was officially steaming.

That does it! I'm gonna wring both of those idiots' stupid turkey necks!

I grabbed my purse, intent on clobbering the pair of clowns with it. But as I started to scoot out of the booth, the waiter came rushing up.

"I'm sorry, ma'am, but you're going to have to leave now. The party who reserved the booth is here."

"That's fine. I was just—"

My voice trailed off. The party with the reservation was standing behind the waiter, staring at me. Dressed in a sharp, tailored suit, I almost didn't recognize him.

But the question was, did *he* recognize *me*?

Chapter Thirty-Seven

"Please, I really need you to vacate the booth immediately, ma'am," the fancy waiter at the Don Cesar said. He leaned forward and whispered, "I'll pay you twenty bucks!"

I hung my head and stared at the tabletop. "Of course. Save your money. I'll be going now."

My heart thumping in my chest, I kept my focus downward and started scooting my satin-lined bowling-ball keister out of the booth. I was almost to the edge when I heard a familiar voice.

"There appears to have been some misunderstanding," he said. "She's with me."

I froze in place.

"Are you *certain* she's with you?" the waiter asked.

All the starch went out of me. I slumped against the back of the bench.

"Yes," Sergeant McNulty said. "Unfortunately, I'm *absolutely* sure."

I was going to jail for sure.

• • • •

"UM, YOU LOOK NICE," I said to McNulty as the waiter stumbled off looking dazed and confused. "Is that suit from Macy's?"

"No." His dark eyes glared a hole through me. "I told you to leave the investigation to *me*!"

"I know! But you have to understand. It's *my* life on the line here! If it were your life at stake, wouldn't you do the same?"

McNulty pursed his lips. "Of course. But there's a difference. I'm a paid professional!"

176

I frowned. "Well, according to Finkerman and Bardsmore, so am I."

"What?"

"Nothing." I bit my bottom lip. "Look. I'm sorry. Why don't you just pick another booth?"

McNulty stared at me like I was from another planet. "Do you think I left all this to chance? I reserved these back-to-back booths as part of my carefully orchestrated plan."

I raised an eyebrow. "Really? Then why'd you just get here?"

The tendons in McNulty's neck flared. "I got caught in traffic, okay? That's the only reason I didn't have the waiter throw you out. I need you to fill me in on what I've missed so far."

I smiled weakly. "In exchange for not arresting me?"

McNulty glared at me. "I absolutely will *not* promise that. Now tell me what you've found out, and I might throw you a little leniency when I book you."

I slumped back in the booth and crossed my arms. "Fine. I learned that those two creeps are misogynist pigs. All they've done is talk about hookers!"

McNulty shook his head. "I *meant* fill me in on anything pertinent to the case."

"Oh." I sat up in the booth. "Well, nothing specific yet. But there *is* one thing I picked up on."

"What?"

"The way Bardsmore is talking about Shamway, I get the feeling he doesn't know Marco's dead."

McNulty tilted his head and leaned toward me. "What did he say that made you assume that?"

"Well, he's talking about Marco in the present tense. About how popular he is with women. How he's loaded with cash, that kind of thing."

McNulty nodded. "Hmm. Okay. Now, no more talking. Shut up and listen. Got it?"

"Got it."

"Here you are, sir," the waiter said as he delivered two sparkling glasses of water to our table, along with a pair of menus in fancy leather covers. As he handed McNulty a menu, I noticed the waiter discreetly slipped the sergeant a piece of paper.

"I'll be back to take your order," the waiter said pleasantly. Then he shot me a slightly horrified glance and disappeared toward the kitchen.

McNulty studied the note, then slid it across the table toward me. It read:

> *I wouldn't touch that one if I were you, sir. Call Mandy's escorts instead. You won't be disappointed! Tell them Brad sent you.*

"What's that all about?" McNulty asked.

I shoved the note back toward him. "How should I know?" I raised my menu up to my eyeballs to hide my red-hot cheeks. "Can I order lunch?"

"Only water and a small salad." McNulty stared at the menu and shook his head. "A full lunch here would cost me half my monthly expense allowance."

"Noted."

McNulty glanced up at me. "Besides, I don't think you could fit another ounce in that lovely dress of yours."

I frowned. I'd heard *that*, too—as much as I didn't want to.

• • • •

"I KNOW!" FINKERMAN'S nasal voice emanated from the booth behind me. "Why don't we use Shamway as eye candy to lure in some hot chicks? Then we can pretend to be hotshots, too. It'll be like shooting girl fish in a barrel."

"Your food, ahem, *gentlemen*," the waiter said. "I must say, it's not often I get a request for raw oysters in the middle of August."

"Nature's aphrodisiac," Finkerman said. "It's gonna come in handy this afternoon for me and my friend here."

"Well, good luck to you both," the waiter said.

I shook my head.

Those two are gonna need a lot more than oysters.

I heard forks begin to clink. Then Bardsmore said, "I've been traveling with Shamway for years. Believe me, his sex appeal doesn't rub off. At least, not on *me* anyway. And between you and me? I'm kind of concerned about the guy."

"STDs?" Finkerman asked.

"Uh ... no. I can't find him. I've been looking for Shamway for three days. He's not in his room. He's not at the bar. He's not even answering his phone. It's like he just fell off the face of the earth."

"See what I mean?" I whispered to McNulty. "Bardsmore doesn't know Shamway's dead!"

McNulty's brow furrowed. "He could just be pretending not to know. Still, it could be legit. Shamway's death hasn't been made public yet."

I raised both eyebrows. "The news isn't public? Why not?"

"For a number of reasons." McNulty sat back and folded his arms across his chest. "We haven't been able to track down his next of kin to notify them first. And we're still trying to determine his actual cause of death."

My nose crinkled. "Are you saying you don't think he was poisoned anymore?"

"The head coroner's been out sick for the past three days. Shamway's been assigned to his understudy. Getting a definite causation is taking longer than usual. But in the meantime, we're working on a new theory."

My face puckered. "Let me guess. Somebody choked Marco to death?"

McNulty's shoulders stiffened. His dark eyes locked on mine. "You really *don't* know when to keep your mouth shut, do you?"

My gut fell four inches. "Oh, no. Don't tell me."

McNulty scowled. "I won't. Now put a lid on it, Fremden. Let me hear what's going on with those two over there."

I nodded solemnly. Then we sat in silence, craning our necks to hear the conversation from the next booth over.

"That's crazy," Finkerman said. "You really can't find your Ferrari, either?"

"No. Somebody stole it yesterday right out of the lot here at the Don."

"Whoa. You think Shamway did it?"

"Doubtful," Bardsmore said. "Like I told you, he's been missing three days. Why would he come back here just to steal my Ferrari?"

"You think he might be dead?" Finkerman asked.

"At this point, who knows?"

"Crap!" Finkerman hissed. "I mean. That would be too bad. But it wouldn't mean we can't go through with the contract for me—I mean my client—to get her 10%, right?"

I crossed my fingers and closed my eyes.

Please universe, please ...

"I wouldn't think so," Bardsmore said. "Shamway signed the paperwork right before he took off. As soon as your client signs, it should be a done deal. Speaking of which, here's the contract."

"Fantastic!" Finkerman practically shouted.

"Yes, it is," I whispered and opened my eyes. McNulty was glaring at me.

Oh, crap. I really am *as stupid as I look.*

"I've got a meeting with my client right after this," Finkerman said. "Afterward, I'll have a courier drop off the signed contract to your room here at the hotel."

"Excellent," Bardsmore said.

Finkerman chuckled gleefully. "Good doing business with you, Bardsmore. Well, I better get going. Good luck finding Shamway."

"Thanks."

"Hey," Finkerman said. "In case there's a problem with the contract and we need Shamway, he didn't mention anyplace he might go while he's here in St. Pete? People he might want to see?"

"No. Not really. Wait a second. Now that you mention it, he told me that while we were here, he wanted to track down some old school chums of his. In fact, your client in particular."

I nearly choked on my $14 side salad. McNulty's eyes bore into me like a pair of ebony drills.

"Did he say why?" Finkerman asked.

"No," Bardsmore said. "Probably to surprise her. You know. With the good news."

"Right," Finkerman said. "Okay, I'll be in touch."

McNulty put a finger to his lips. "They're getting up. Keep quiet and act casual."

I nodded, trying desperately not to cough as I strangled on a clump of salad lodged in my throat.

As Finkerman stood, I felt the booth shift under me. I dared a glance his way and saw him take a step in our direction. Then, for some reason, Finkerman stopped and turned back, leaving me with an unseemly view of the ass-end of his gnarly blue leisure suit.

"Oh," Finkerman said. "I almost forgot. What's your room number?"

"Thirty-nine," Bardsmore said.

I gasped, dislodging a chunk of tomato wedged in my throat. It skittered across the table and landed in a globby heap on McNulty's half-eaten dinner roll.

He shook his head. "Fremden, you are the biggest—"

"Shh!" I shushed McNulty, then climbed up on my knees and peeked over the back of the booth. I couldn't believe my eyes.

Just as I suspected.

I wasn't the only one disguising themselves as someone else.

Chapter Thirty-Eight

Choking on my salad, I turned, sat back in the booth, and swatted at Sergeant McNulty like a deranged cat trying to catch a feather duster.

"What's wrong with you?" he hissed. "I told you to act casual. Not crazy!"

I grabbed my dinner napkin and coughed into it. Another chunk of tomato flew out. I sucked in a lungful of air and squealed, "Stop him! Don't let him leave!"

McNulty shook his head. "I know you want your money, Fremden. But sink your greedy claws into Finkerman *after* he leaves the restaurant. If he and Bardsmore see me here, my investigation will be compromised."

"No," I whispered. "Not Finkerman. *Bardsmore.* He's not Bardsmore!"

"I know that," McNulty said. "Bardsmore's dead. This guy's an imposter."

"I know!"

McNulty's eyebrows met. "Then what are you talking about?"

I grabbed my glass of water and took a sip. The last of the tomato finally slid down my throat.

"Listen," I gasped. "I met the guy claiming to be Anthony Bardsmore at the pool a couple of days ago. Only he told me his name was *Don McLester!*"

McNulty frowned. "Does he know who *you* are?"

"No. I told him my name was Thelma."

McNulty shook his head. "Classic. You lied about your name. He lied about his. People do it all the time. It's not a crime, per se."

A significant bit of starch went out of my sails. I sat back in the booth. "I guess you're right. But why would he bother to lie to *me*?"

McNulty's dark eyes studied me carefully. "Why would you bother to lie to *him*?"

"I ... uh ...," I stammered.

McNulty's lips curled into a sour smirk. "Let me guess. He thought you were a prostitute, didn't he?"

I cringed. "Damn. You really *are* a good detective."

• • • •

AFTER PAYING THE BILL, McNulty gave me my marching orders. I was to stay out of his investigation, or else. But he also let me know he'd be taking a closer look at Don McLester, aka Anthony Bardsmore. So, there was *that* ...

And then there was something even better. As soon as I found Finkerman and signed on the dotted line, I'd be a millionaire.

Despite looking like a low-rent call girl, I left the Don Cesar restaurant with a grin on my face and a swagger in my step. My prospects had gone from *America's Most Wanted* to *Lifestyles of the Rich and Famous* in under an hour.

Not bad for a drag queen bingo reject.

• • • •

AS I PULLED SHABBY Maggie up to the lot attendant's booth on my way out of the Don Cesar parking lot, I took a chance and asked the squirrelly little guy inside about Bardsmore's missing red Ferrari.

To my surprise, he winked at me, then laughed. "Happens a lot more than you think."

My mouth fell open. "You mean thieves regularly steal cars right out of this lot?"

"No way!" He laughed. "Not thieves. *Repo men*." Above his sunglasses, the kid's blond eyebrows wagged. "They pay me a hundred large to let them in so they can repo these deadbeats' fancy rides. Karmic justice for the little guy, am I right?"

"Uh ... sure." I shot him a tentative smile, then punched the gas.

As I pulled onto Gulf Boulevard, I wondered why Bardsmore—aka McLester – or whoever he was, didn't make his car payment. It couldn't be a money issue. As personal attorney for Marco Shamway, the guy had to be loaded. Right?

Unless Marco had screwed *him* over the same way he had *me*.

OMG. That's it!

Shamway isn't paying his attorney what he owes him. That's a motive for murder, isn't it?

I glanced around, intent on finding a spot to pull over and call McNulty with the news. The moment I took my foot off the gas, a horn blared behind me.

"Seriously?" I grumbled and glared into the rearview mirror, searching for the impatient jerk who'd honked at me for slowing down.

That's when I caught a flash of something rusty and orange coming up fast in the lane behind me. It was Finkerman in his ratty old Gremlin, waving for me to pull over. The heap of junk he was driving was smoking harder than a death-row inmate after finishing his last meal.

"What does *he* want?" I muttered. Then I remembered. My million-dollar contract. Oh, yeah. *That's* what.

Ka-ching!

Chapter Thirty-Nine

I hooked a sharp right into the parking lot of the Circle-J.

Finkerman pulled up behind me, then came racing up to my window. He leaned over and opened his mouth to speak, then shrunk back as if I'd just sprayed him with mace.

"Ack! Who are you?" he demanded. "Did you steal this car?"

I pushed the bangs of the ratty auburn wig away from my eyes. "No, Finkerman. It's *me*."

"Fremden?" His freckled nose crinkled. "What the hell happened to you?"

"Long story. Not important at the moment."

He held up an open palm. "Okay. Fine. Whatever floats your boat. We all gotta eat."

"What?" I hissed. "No, it's not what it looks like," I tried to explain. But Finkerman didn't hear me. He was too busy making a mad dash to the passenger side of my car.

He opened the door and climbed into the seat beside me. "Now, about the meeting—"

"Wait," I said. "I have a question first. Why would a rich person let their Ferrari be repossessed?"

Finkerman frowned. Then he smiled. It was the same smile I'd made when I'd seen that Snidely Whiplash moustache scrawled across Marco's face on that billboard.

"You're talking about Bardsmore, eh?" he said, then chuckled. "What a shyster. The world is full of posers, Fremden. Don't you know that by now? They live paycheck to paycheck. Or, should I say, thanks to today's technology, they live direct deposit to direct deposit."

I pursed my lips. "You think Bardsmore's broke?"

Finkerman shrugged. "I'm an attorney, not an accountant. But I know this. A lot of so-called rich folks are leveraged up to their hundred-dollar haircuts. It wouldn't surprise me if

Bardsmore was one of them. The guy's a total dumbass. I'll prove it to you."

Finkerman flipped open his battered briefcase.

I grimaced. "Uh ... about the contract. It doesn't matter if Shamway's dead, does it?"

He grinned. "Not a whit! Not unless you killed—" Finkerman's eyes grew as big as boiled eggs. "Wait. Is Shamway dead for real?"

I nodded.

"How do you know—" Finkerman's pasty face crumbled. "Aww, no! Don't tell me the dead guy you hit in the head with a hammer was Marco Shamway!"

I cringed. "Okay. I won't tell you."

• • • •

AFTER I FINALLY GOT Finkerman to stop crying, I explained to him that I really, truly, honest-to-God didn't kill Marco Shamway. I also told him that McNulty was looking into Don McLester (aka Bardsmore) as a possible suspect.

"So, there's still a chance you didn't do it?" Finkerman asked, wiping tears from his freckled face with a grubby hanky.

"More than a chance. It's 100% true."

Finkerman blew his nose, then instantly perked up, as if someone had pushed his reset button. "Well, all right then. Let's get this puppy signed!" He popped open his briefcase again.

"Okay. But I have to say, I'm disappointed in you. I thought you were going to try to negotiate for a higher percentage."

Finkerman froze, then turned his beady eyes on me. "How do you know I *didn't*?"

Oops.

"Uh ... past lousy service?"

Finkerman shrugged, then grinned again. "Well, have no fears, Fremden. As it turned out, I didn't *need* to negotiate."

187

I frowned. "What are you talking about?"

Finkerman shoved the contract in my face and pointed to a spot in the bottom left corner with a long, ghostly finger. "Check this out. There's a typo on your royalty share. Instead of 10%, it's 100%!"

"What?" I gasped.

Finkerman giggled with glee. "Some idiot added an extra zero by mistake." He smirked and tapped his temple with his index finger. "But old Finkerman kept his cool. I didn't say a word to Bardsmore, and he didn't catch the error. Ha! I told you he was a dumbass!"

I grimaced. "But that means the contract needs to be corrected before it's valid, doesn't it?"

"Are you *kidding*?" Finkerman squirmed in the seat next to me like a kid about to pee his pants. "Fremden, once you sign this bad boy, it's as unretractable as my ex-wife's restraining order!"

I chewed my bottom lip. "I don't know about this..."

Slowly and carefully, Finkerman set the contract on the dashboard as if it were made of Tiffany glass. Then he lunged at me, grabbed me by the shoulders, and shook me like a ragdoll.

"Get ahold of yourself!" he screeched in my face. "You're staring at *karmic justice* here, Fremden! Shamway's already signed the documents. As soon as you put your John Hancock on the line, the entire Hunk Clock fortune is yours!" He stopped shaking me. "Minus my 20%, of course."

My heart thumped wildly in my chest. "But ... but ... wouldn't that be fraud?"

"Nope. It's all perfectly legal, as far as you know."

"I dunno ..."

Finkerman slapped a pen in my hand, then grabbed the contract from the dashboard and held it in front of me. "Sign it, Fremden. Sign it now before you have a heart attack, or get shot or something!"

I glanced around. "Who's gonna shoot me here in the Circle-J parking lot?"

"*I* am—if you don't sign this bloody contract *right now!*"

"All right, already!" I clicked open the pen. As my hand was poised over the contract, my fingers began to tremble.

All I have to do is sign my name on the dotted line and my life will be golden.

Go on, Val! Sign it! What are you waiting for?

I don't know. It feels wrong somehow.

Are you kidding me?

Damn my stupid, useless personal integrity! Why did it always have to kick in at the worst possible moments?

I pulled the pen away. "Sorry, Finkerman. I need some time to think about this."

Finkerman stared at me as if I'd just morphed into a brain-eating zombie before his very eyes.

"What?" he screeched and waved the contract in my face. "What in the world is there to think about? Shamway ruined your life. Paybacks are hell. Here's your chance to stick it to him while he can't fight back!"

I stared at the contract.

Should I or shouldn't I?

I'd stolen money out of Geraldine's cash register. So technically, I was already a criminal.

Wait. What if crime is my true calling in life? That would make so much sense, considering what a failure I've been at everything else ...

"Come *on*, Fremden!" Finkerman begged. "What are you waiting for? If the tables were turned, Shamway would do the same to you in a heartbeat! What am I saying? The guy *already has*! Besides, he doesn't need the money anymore. He's dead. It might as well go to you and me, right?"

I swallowed hard. Then I uttered a phrase I'd have bet my life I'd never say in a million years.

"Finkerman, you're right."

Chapter Forty

I'd just pulled up to Belated Rooms when my cell phone rang. It was Sergeant McNulty.

"Are you sitting down?" he asked.

I wiggled my sweaty, satin-covered butt against Maggie's red pleather seat. "Yeah. Why?"

"I just ran the report on Don McLester. The guy's been a con artist since the age of thirteen."

I gasped. "Are you saying he's not even a real attorney? Aww, crap!" My gut fell into my thrift-store stilettos. My beautiful mountain of Hunk Clock money had just turned into a heap of cow dung.

"No. I didn't say that," McNulty said.

I shot up in my seat and squeezed my cell phone so hard it should've shattered. "Then McLester *is* a real attorney?"

"Yes."

"Thank the lord!"

"Excuse me?" McNulty said. "Thank the lord?"

I cringed. "Uh ... I was just thinking of poor Marco and the other people McLester might've ripped off if he'd been a fake attorney."

"Uh-huh."

I took a deep breath and tried to sound breezy. "By the way, hypothetically, if McLester *did* kill Marco, would he be disbarred?"

"Undoubtedly."

Crap!

"Would it be retroactive?" I asked as my emotions flip-flopped between elation and despair. "You know, like if he'd represented certain clients in a deal before they found out he'd killed someone—"

"What on earth are you rambling on about, Fremden?"

I slumped back into my seat. "Nothing."

Goodbye caviar dreams and champagne wishes.

"Tell me why you think McLester killed Shamway," McNulty said. "Besides the obvious reason that it would get you off the hook."

I frowned and set my jaw to determined. My boat hadn't come in, but I wasn't going down alone on the ship. "Marco shafted me over the Hunk Clock. Why couldn't he have done the same to McLester? Like I said before, he who controls the paperwork ends up with all the paper money."

"Fair point," McNulty said. "McLester certainly has the track record for dirty dealings. But fraud and larceny are a far cry from murder. He's never committed a violent crime. At least, not one we're aware of."

"Well, there's a first time for everything," I said.

"Yes," McNulty said slowly. "I suppose you would know all about that."

I closed my eyes and shook my head.

When will I ever learn to shut up?

After a long pause McNulty said, "Anyway, the reason I called was to let you know that McLester definitely warrants further investigation. Tell me, Fremden. Exactly how did you get tangled up with this guy in the first place? At the pool when he thought you were a prostitute?"

"No. The day before that. McLester came by my house and left a business card for Anthony Bardsmore in my front door."

"Who told you that?" McNulty asked.

"No one. I was home. I saw him myself."

"Are you sure it was McLester? Can you testify to it?"

I grimaced. "I want to say yes. But honestly, he was wearing a baseball cap pulled down low over his face. I'm pretty sure it was him. Same basic body shape."

"Hold on. Why didn't you answer the door?"

I grimaced. "I was indisposed."

"Indisposed?"

Angry. Paranoid. Groggy. A little bit drunk. Take your pick.

"It's personal," I said. "But the guy was also driving a red Ferrari, just like the one Bardsmore said was stolen from the Don Cesar parking lot."

"Hmm," McNulty said. "McLester could've stolen the vehicle from Bardsmore."

"Not likely. The lot attendant told me the Ferrari had been repossessed."

"Did he now?" McNulty's tone shifted a notch higher. "How'd you get him to tell you that?"

"I have my feminine ways."

"Don't tell me you—never mind. I don't want to know."

"Geez! Nothing like that," I grumbled. "Like I told you before, when I met him at the pool, McLester told me he was staying in room 39. That's the same room Bardsmore told Finkerman at lunch today."

"Yes," McNulty said. "Well, at least I know where I can find him for questioning."

"Exactly."

Suddenly a thought hit me. "Oh my lord! That means McLester *knows where I live!*"

"That just occurred to you?" McNulty said.

Apparently so.

"It makes sense now," I said. "McLester could've come back to my place sometime after dropping off the business card identifying him as Bardsmore and stolen my Hammer of Justice from my garage—so he could frame me for Shamway's murder!"

"To what end?" McNulty asked.

"I don't know. You're the detective!"

"You're picking *now* to actually follow my lead?"

I frowned. "Maybe McLester didn't want me to get a piece of the Hunk Clock fortune. Maybe Shamway owed him a ton of money and McLester figured the only way he'd get paid was to kill Shamway and fudge the paperwork so he'd inherit the whole thing for himself."

"Let's not get ahead of ourselves, Fremden. Even if you're right, we're only talking about a 10% stake in the business. McLester would still be able to steal 90% without having to frame you for Shamway's murder. Now, if you'd been given the lion's share, *that* might be an entirely different story."

"Uh ... right."

"You sound strange," McNulty said. "Is there something you're not telling me?"

"Not that you're aware of."

"Fremden?"

I clicked off the phone. My head was spinning. By signing that fraudulent 100% royalty share contract with Finkerman, had I just sealed my own fate? Had I just moved into the bullseye of McLester's plan to target me for Marco's murder? Or, worse yet, was I now 90% more likely to become McLester's next murder victim?

I had to undo the damage before anyone found out!

Hands trembling, I called Finkerman.

"It's a fine day for a Finker—"

"Shut up and give me McLester's number!"

"No way, Fremden."

I blanched. "What? Why not?"

"Because I know you," Finkerman said. "You'll do something stupid. You'll ruin the deal!"

"But ... but .... Gimme that number or I'll fire you and you won't get a dime!"

Finkerman laughed. "Too late. I'm at the courthouse now."

I frowned. "So?"

"So, you'll never get here before I file the paperwork. Sorry, Fremden, but this baby's a done deal."

"What? Ugh! Finkerman, you suck!"

Chapter Forty-One

Parked outside Belated Rooms, I sat inside my old Ford Falcon and contemplated my life. For a gal with not much going on, I had a hell of a lot going on.

Murder suspect. Drag queen impersonator. Contract fraudster. Thieving thrift-store flunky. Sketchy girlfriend. And now, murder target of Don McLester.

Through the side mirror, I glanced up at the movie marquee across the street. The new flick playing was *That Time I Kinda Killed a Guy*.

I winced. From where I sat, it was more like *That Time I Kinda Got Killed by a Guy*. If I was right about McLester, I was worth a hell of a lot more to him dead than alive.

"Come in out of the heat, Hun!" I heard a voice call out.

My eyes shifted from the side mirror to the windshield. There, standing before me, was Laverne in her gold lamé pantsuit. Good thing she wasn't McLester or I'd have been a dead duck. I never saw her coming.

"Honey, you're gonna roast alive in that car," she called, beckoning me with a wave. "Get in here. I've got a surprise for you!"

Geez. I sure hope it's not McLester.

I got out and followed Laverne into Belated Rooms. Once inside, I was surprised to see an old lady rifling through the cash register.

"Laverne, you're supposed to be watching the till!" I said.

"She was," the old woman at the register said. "Which is more than I can say for you." She looked up. It was Geraldine Jiggles, looking fly in a sequined top and matching visor. Apparently, she'd lost both her shirt and her skunk stripe at the slots back in Vegas.

"Where have you been?" she asked. "Hosting drag queen bingo?"

I grimaced. I guess it was my turn to look like a washed-up Vegas showgirl. "It's complicated."

"Sounds like it," Geraldine said. "Lulu told me all about your little spy mission."

I cringed. "I wouldn't have left work except for—"

"Oh, save it, Fremden," Geraldine said. "I figured you wouldn't work hard. But at least you *did* work smart." She turned and smiled at Laverne. "Turns out Lulu here is a natural-born saleswoman. She just talked a tourist into buying a down jacket in case the weather turns cold!"

Laverne giggled. "It was easy. The lady told me she was a snowbird, so I figured that jacket would come in handy."

I just stood there, mouth open. My current reality—for numerous reasons—was just too surreal to take in.

"Anything interesting happen while I was gone?" Geraldine asked. "Besides the crazy crap you've got going on, I mean."

Laverne might've spilled the beans, but she didn't know about me being a prime suspect for Marco's murder. I wanted to keep it that way. "Uh, Laverne? I'm back, so you're free to go."

"Really?" Laverne's pug eyes darted in the direction of the washroom. "Okay. I guess I could go give it the old showgirl try!" She turned and skittered off toward the restroom.

Geraldine laughed. "That gal's a piece of work."

"You have no idea."

"So, what's been going on around here while I was gone?"

There was no use hiding my predicament from the hardened old woman. She'd seen it all, so I decided to come clean. "I found something in the alley the day you left."

"Huh." Geraldine shrugged and continued counting the money in the till. "You don't say."

I tried to read her reaction, but the woman had a poker face that could probably fool even McNulty. "Aren't you curious what I found?"

"Not really," Geraldine said. "You forget. I've worked here a hell of a lot longer than you have. By the way, where's my hammer? I'm pretty sure I left it in the storeroom."

"The police took it for evidence."

Still no reaction, other than I thought I saw one of Geraldine's eyebrows tick up a notch.

"Why?" she asked nonchalantly.

"Because I hit the dead guy in the head with it."

Geraldine flinched ever so slightly. "Damn, Fremden. That was my lucky hammer. I'm gonna have to take it out of your pay."

"Seriously?" I hissed. "I'm accused of murdering this guy and you're worried about a twenty-dollar hammer?"

"Murder?" Geraldine's eyes widened a bit. "You never said anything about murder."

"Yes, *murder*! And the police have me targeted as the main suspect!"

In the heat of the moment, I hadn't noticed Laverne return from the restroom. I heard her burst into tears behind me.

"Oh, Honey," she wailed. "I knew that terrible habit of yours was going to do you in one day!"

I turned around to face her. "Laverne! I didn't kill anybody, I swear!"

"She's telling the truth," Geraldine said. She walked over and put an arm around Laverne. "That poor sap was already dead before Fremden ever set foot in the alley."

I nearly choked on my own saliva. "*What*? I've been going crazy trying to prove I didn't do it! Why didn't you call the cops when you found him?"

Geraldine shrugged. "I didn't want them messing up my trip to Vegas with all their stupid questions."

"So you set me up for the fall instead?"

"Nope," Geraldine said. "You did that all by yourself."

My shoulders slumped. "That's what I don't understand. How did my Hammer of Justice get inside the box with him?"

Laverne cringed. "I did it, Val. I slipped it inside one of J.D.'s boxes before we brought the stuff here." She burst into tears again. "I wanted to save you from yourself. But I just made it all worse!"

"You didn't make it worse," I lied, patting her on the back. "I didn't kill the guy with my hammer or anybody else's. Besides, now the cops think somebody might've choked him to death."

"If that's the case, accusing you of it is malarkey," Geraldine said.

I brightened a bit at the old woman's confidence in me. "Thank you."

"Eh," Geraldine said. "Judging by how this place looks, you don't have the strength to push a broom around, much less wring a full-grown man's neck."

My smile soured. "Again, thank you. Now, could you do me a favor and come with me to the police station and explain all of this to Sergeant McNulty?"

Geraldine frowned. "Who'll mind the store?"

I blanched. "You're worried about five bucks in sales while my life is hanging here in the balance?"

Geraldine's beady eyes narrowed. "Speaking of balance, there appears to be $45 dollars missing from the till."

My face went slack. "How can you know—. Ugh! Never mind that for now! I'll pay it back, already."

"Why don't we work it out in trade?" Geraldine said. "How about you pull another shift tomorrow and we'll call it even?"

I groaned. "Abandon hope all ye who enter here."

Geraldine laughed. "You sound just like Jerry. He was always writing notes like that."

I frowned. "What happened to him?"

"He sent me a text. He and Lily are headed to Vegas."

"To gamble?"

"Yeah. They're getting married."

Man, you got that *right.*

"Come on, let's go," I said, and headed for the door. Geraldine didn't budge. "Laverne can mind the store. Right Laverne?"

"Uh, sure, Honey," Laverne said. "But maybe you want to change first? Looks like your dress popped a seam."

Geraldine shook her head. "Or at least ditch that ridiculous wig, toots. Haven't you heard? Vaudeville is dead."

Chapter Forty-Two

"This information is helpful, but it still doesn't clear you, Fremden," McNulty said, his eyes on Geraldine as we sat across the interrogation table from him. "And as for you, Ms. Jiggles, if you weren't a senior citizen, I'd book you right now for failure to report a death."

Geraldine shot me some side-eye. "See? That's why I didn't call it in in the first place. If I had, I'd have never made the plane to Vegas, much less hit it big on the slots."

"How big?" McNulty asked.

Geraldine smirked. "You a player? I took 'em for over fifty grand."

"Impressive." McNulty leaned in and smiled softly. "Care to make a wager with me?"

Geraldine's smirk vanished and her eyes narrowed. "What did you have in mind?"

"Hold on." McNulty left, then returned a moment later holding a woman's oversized pocketbook. He set it on the table. "Lift that, and I'll give you fifty bucks."

"Huh?" I grunted.

"You're on!" Geraldine shot to standing, rubbed her hands together, then picked up the purse with one hand. "Ha! Pay up, sucker!"

McNulty smiled. "Well, I'll be."

"Wait!" I practically hollered. "I want a turn!"

My flat-broke ass sprang out of the chair. I grinned triumphantly, grabbed the purse handle and tugged. It stuck to the table like it had been superglued.

"What the?" I muttered, then yanked on the purse so hard I nearly threw my back out. Still nothing. Not even a wiggle. I flopped back into my chair defeated.

Geez! Outdone by an old lady? Maybe I'm as lazy as Geraldine says I am!

"You're one strong lady," McNulty said to Geraldine. "You work out with magnets?"

She shrugged. "Naw. Mostly free weights."

I shook my head. "What are you two talking about?"

McNulty smiled smugly. "Ms. Jiggles here has the upper body strength of a twenty-year-old weightlifter." He studied Geraldine. "You see, I moved here from Vegas. I've seen this kind of thing before."

"Vegas is full of super-strong old ladies?" I asked.

"No, not full," McNulty said. "But there are a few. They carry around huge magnets in their purses, just like this one. I brought it with me as a souvenir from one I caught out there."

"It's illegal for old ladies to carry magnets?" I asked, still confused.

"Ask your friend there, Fremden," McNulty said. "It's a con. They put the magnet in front of slot machines to scramble their mechanisms into hitting the jackpot."

I stared at Geraldine with newfound respect. "Wow."

"I bet your check-on luggage was a fifty-pound magnet," McNulty said to Geraldine.

She scoffed. "Don't be ridiculous. I'd never have been able to get that through airport security nowadays."

"Of course," McNulty said. "You bought it while you were there."

The old lady shrugged. "More like borrowed. Those magnets ain't cheap."

"But well worth the return on investment," McNulty said.

"What's the harm?" Geraldine grumbled. "Those casinos take enough of our hard-earned money. Besides, it's not a crime if you don't get caught, right?"

"But it is if you *do*."

We sat there in silence as McNulty studied first Geraldine, then me. "This all makes sense now," he said as he rubbed his chin and nodded slowly.

"What makes sense?" I asked.

"The M.O.," McNulty said. "Choking Shamway to death wasn't a one-woman job. It took the both of you."

Chapter Forty-Three

Without enough evidence to book us for murder, McNulty settled on lesser charges. Desecration of a corpse for me. Failure to report a death for Geraldine. On the bright side, thanks to winning big in Vegas, Geraldine was able to post both of our bonds.

We were free for the moment. But how long would that last?

On the way back to Belated Rooms, I filled Geraldine in on everything that had gone on while she was away. By the time we reached Corey Avenue, the wily old woman was up to speed on every detail about Marco Shamway's death, the sketchy royalty contract for the Hunk Clock, and McLester's plan to frame me for Marco's murder—or possibly target me for his second victim.

"That's quite a tale," Geraldine said as I dropped her off in front of the thrift shop. "You managed to do all that in three days?"

"Yeah. When it comes to being a crap magnet, I'm an overachiever."

"You aren't kidding."

"Look," I said. "Thanks again for bailing me out. I promise I'll pay you back."

Geraldine opened the door to get out, then turned back toward me. "Don't sweat it, kid." Her gentle tone and the way she patted my hand reminded me of a kindly little old granny. But then I caught a disconcerting gleam in her eye that set me on edge.

As she shut the door and headed for Belated Rooms, I began to wonder. What did I actually know about Geraldine Jiggles? Only that she was an ex Vegas showgirl, a greedy slots cheat, a mercenary thrift shop owner, and strong enough to snap me like a twig.

I shifted into reverse and pulled out of the parking spot. As I headed down Corey Avenue, my mind swirled with questions.

Geraldine was a hard-boiled cheapskate. Why had she suddenly offered to post my bail? Was she lying to McNulty? Had *she* actually throttled Shamway to death? If so, what was in it for her to pony up the money so I could go free?

As I pulled up to a stop sign, a thought hit me like a bullet between the eyes.

Geraldine and McLester were both con artists. What if they knew each other? What if they were working together to defraud Shamway of his Hunk Clock fortune?

And what if the only thing left standing in their way was *me*?

Chapter Forty-Four

T he sun was setting when I pulled up into my driveway.

But instead of admiring the golden glow, all I could think about was that there might be a price on my head. McLester or some hitman he hired could be lurking inside my house right now, getting ready to snuff me out to clear the way for him to inherit Marco's fortune.

A shiver ran through me as I sat there in the growing dusk. It would be dark soon. And with Tom gone, I'd be all alone in the house overnight. Why oh why did he have to be gone when I needed him most?

I glanced around the yard. Except for the glowing eyes of Laverne's yard gnomes next door, the coast seemed clear. I scrambled out of my car and raced my imaginary killers up to the front door.

I shoved the key in the lock and was about to turn it when a bolt of paranoia shot through me.

What if McLester and his goons are already inside?

The hair on the back of my neck stood up. Wild-eyed, I glanced around for a weapon. The only thing I could find was a terracotta pot. I grabbed it, shook the poor dead plant out, and crept inside my house.

After peeking inside every closet, under every bed, and behind every door and shower curtain, I felt relatively certain no murderers were lying in wait inside.

I set the pot down on the kitchen counter and got busy making sure every window and door was locked. Satisfied I was alone, I grabbed Tom's last beer from the fridge and hit the flashing red light on the answering machine.

A message came on. But it was just a few seconds of static. I checked the number of the caller. It didn't look familiar. Unable to stop myself, I hit redial. It rang once, then a recording came on saying the number had been disconnected.

Who would call my landline and not leave a message? A telemarketer or a murderer, that's who!

I threw back another slug of liquid courage, then padded into the second bedroom that I used as an office. Inside was a daybed, and a small desk and chair. The desk was outfitted with a computer and a jar full of jellybeans.

I'd been using the computer to write newspaper and magazine articles. The jellybeans were a reward for completing whatever goal I'd set for myself for the day. Sometimes the goal was finishing an article. Sometimes for sending one to a publisher. Other times, for just sitting in the chair and trying. (As they say, inspiration comes when it will.)

I'd actually had a few articles published. One in a newspaper in Lakeland, Florida. Another in a coupon-saver rag. My latest had been a human-interest story featuring a woman and her pet pig. I'd sent it in to the *Beach Gazette* but had yet to hear back. Not even with a lousy rejection letter.

Not that it mattered financially. What I'd gotten paid for the first two articles wouldn't have bought a case of the beer I was chugging.

I eyed the jar of jellybeans.

Screw it. What am I saving them for? I could wake up dead tomorrow!

I popped a handful of jellybeans into my mouth. As I bit down on them, I finally remembered what I'd come in my office for in the first place—my high-school yearbook.

I scanned the bookshelf and pulled it from the shelf. Then I padded to my bedroom, yearbook, and jellybeans in tow. I changed into a nightgown, climbed into bed, and put on my ever-reliable nighttime sleep aid, *Forensic Files*.

All settled in, I cracked open the book. There he was on the first page, leaning against a tree looking like a teenage Adonis. Marco Shamway. Class president. Idea thief.

Destroyer of dreams. And now, through no fault of his own, unwitting financier of my untimely demise.

Chapter Forty-Five

I*t was some kind of miracle. I was skinny and my thighs
didn't wobble!*

*I was a teenager again. Milly and I were at Sunset Beach
along with our classmates for our senior class beach
blowout. Everyone was giddy with excitement. In a few days
we would all graduate and be let loose on the world!*

*The jocks were playing beach volleyball. The cute girls
were sunbathing. The popular kids were in the Gulf,
splashing and bobbing on floats.*

As for me? I was running for my life.

*As usual, Marco Shamway had singled me out for his
special brand of humiliation. The handsome jerk was chasing
me along the shoreline wielding a blue crab.*

*I squealed with terror as he drew ever nearer, taunting
me with its pinchers. "I'm gonna get you, Val Fremden!"*

*Suddenly I tripped and tumbled across the sugar-white
sand. Marco overtook me. I could feel his hot breath on me
as he bent over and brushed a claw against my cheek ...*

• • • •

I WOKE WITH A START. Thank goodness it had all been a
dream!

But in the dim, pinkish light of dawn, I saw the outline of
a man standing over my bedside.

"Tom?" I asked.

"No," he said. "Guess again."

Chapter Forty-Six

I recognized the intruder's voice. It was Don McLester.

"What are you doing here?" I squealed, my heart suddenly pounding in my throat.

"Relax," he said. "I have a little proposition for you."

Proposition? Since when is murder a proposition?

"You can have the royalties," I blurted. "I won't say a thing!"

"Royalties?" He laughed.

I pulled the sheets up to my neck. "Aren't you here to kill me for the Hunk Clock fortune?"

He sat on the edge of the bed beside me. His ample girth caused the bedsprings to let out a painful *squeak*.

"After I saw you at the pool the other day, I couldn't stop thinking about you," he said. "I find you attractive. Any chance you might be interested in an old geezer like me?"

What the hell?

I sat up in bed and glanced around in the dim light for something to defend myself with. The only things within my reach were an empty jellybean jar and my high-school yearbook. Unfortunately, neither seemed suitable weapons against a horny walrus.

Then I remembered a tactic used by survivors on *Forensic Files* and thought, *If I play my cards right, I just might get out of this alive ...*

I forced myself to giggle and smile at McLester. "Well, of course I'm interested in you," I said as casually as I could muster. "Breaking and entering isn't exactly the most romantic way to a woman's heart, but it certainly gets a girl's attention."

McLester smiled. "In your line of work, I figured you'd be used to strange men showing up at all hours, *Thelma*."

"Uh, sure," I said. "That's the life of a busy call girl."

"I was hoping to take you away from all that. Make an honest woman of you."

Seriously? As I recall you told Finkerman you'd rather drive off a cliff than sleep with me.

"Wow," I said, feigning gratitude. "That sounds like an interesting proposition indeed."

McLester beamed. "Right? Given your age and condi—"

"Quick question," I said, cutting him off. "How did you figure out where I live?"

McLester cocked his hammy head and shrugged. "Anybody with an internet connection can find *that* out."

"Oh."

"So, what do you say, Sweet Cheeks?" McLester asked. "Think you could learn to love a guy like me?"

He pushed me back on the bed and leaned forward to kiss me. It took all the strength I had not to grimace.

As he closed in, I smiled sweetly and wrapped my fingers around the jellybean jar.

Then he wrapped his fingers around my throat!

Suddenly, I knew exactly what had happened to Marco Shamway.

I just had to live long enough to prove it.

Chapter Forty-Seven

I smiled up at McLester's jowly face hovering inches from my own. "Honey," I said sweetly, "if you want a real relationship, we should take it a little slower, don't you think?"

McLester took his hands from my throat and sat up. I almost exploded with relief.

"Slower?" he asked.

"Yes. We should go out on a date."

"A date?"

"Absolutely," I said. "That way we can get to know each other better. Everybody knows you don't have sex on a first date if you want it to last."

McLester frowned. "Oh. Well, I guess it wouldn't hurt anything."

"Exactly!" I said a tad too enthusiastically. I squirmed around him and got out of bed.

"Where are you going?" he asked.

"To the bathroom to get ready. I want you to take me out to breakfast. How's that sound?"

"Okay, I guess."

"Perfect!" Forcing myself not to run, I made it out of the bedroom. Once out of McLester's view, I bolted into the kitchen, grabbed my cell phone from the counter, and fled into the bathroom. I locked the door behind me, climbed into the tub, and called Sergeant McNulty.

"Fremden? It's Sunday morning. This better be good."

"I need your help!" I whispered. "McLester broke into my place. He's here right now!"

"What? Are you in danger? I'll arrange a SWAT team!"

"No. No cop cars. I want you to meet me at the Friendly Fish Café for their Sunday breakfast buffet."

"What? That doesn't make any sense."

"Please. Trust me on this. I'll explain everything when I see you there."

McLester knocked on the bathroom door. "Everything okay in there?"

"Yes!" I called out. "Just making myself gorgeous for you!"

"I get the situation," McNulty said. "Be careful, Fremden. If you're not at the restaurant in ten minutes, I'm heading to your house."

"Thank you," I whispered. "I gotta go."

Chapter Forty-Eight

"**T**here you are!" I said as McNulty entered the restaurant. I let go of McLester's sweaty hand, jumped up out of the booth, and ran over to greet him.

I kissed McNulty on the cheek and whispered, "You're my pimp. Just go with it."

McNulty, to his credit, didn't even blink. "You're okay?"

"Yes."

"What's your plan?"

"To get him to confess."

"But—"

I whirled around and beamed at McLester. "Honey, before we can really start dating, I need you to meet my ... er ... *manager*. I needed a name for McNulty, but my mind went blank. I searched around wildly for some kind of inspiration. "Uh ... this is ... uh ... Heinz Pickleworth."

McLester laughed. "That's quite a name for someone in your profession."

McNulty slid into the booth opposite McLester and me. "It's an old family name my mother always relished."

McLester laughed again. "Quick on your feet. I can see why Thelma speaks highly of you." He patted my thigh.

I giggled and wondered if I had enough bleach to take a bath in once I got home. I locked eyes with McNulty. "I was telling Don that while he was in town, he simply couldn't miss the world-famous shrimp and grits at the Friendly Fish!"

"Right," McNulty said. "What brings you into town in the first place, Don?"

He smirked smugly. "Business. You seen the billboards for the Hunk Clock? That's my client, Marco Shamway."

"Wow," McNulty said. "Impressive. It's a real shame about Marco passing away."

"He's *dead*?" McLester asked. "I had no idea. The guy was my best client ... and a dear friend."

I shook my head. "I always had a crush on Marco. If he were still alive, I'd jump his bones. I can't believe someone murdered him."

McLester grimaced. "He was murdered?"

McNulty shot me a *what the hell's going on* look and cleared his throat. "Well, not exactly," he said. "I got the final cause of death from the coroner's office last night. It turns out Shamway wasn't actually murdered. He appears to have died due to anaphylactic shock. He had a mouthful of undigested shrimp salad in his gut."

"What!" McLester gasped. "I had no idea he was allergic to shellfish."

"It appears Shamway didn't know either, or he didn't realize what he was eating."

I frowned and glanced around the Friendly Fish. "They were serving shrimp salad here on Thursday. It was the daily special. Wait. It was also the special on Wednesday, too."

"Your thrift shop is just a half a block from here," McNulty said. "Shamway could've taken a bite of the sandwich, stumbled down the alley, then fallen into the box outside your back door and died before anyone could help him."

"Poor bastard," McLester said.

"Oh. It's you again," the waitress said, coming up to the table with our menus.

I thought she was talking to me, but her eyes were on McLester.

"Where's your cute pal?" she asked. "He took off so quick the other day I never got to give him my number."

McNulty's eyes locked on McLester. "You were here with Shamway?"

"Yeah. But—"

"What day was he here with this other man?" McNulty asked the waitress.

She tapped a pen on her notepad. "Wednesday. They both had the shrimp salad sandwich."

"Are you certain?" McNulty asked.

"I'm sure," she said. "Honey, when you see a handsome hunk like the guy this lump was sitting with, you don't forget him."

McLester grimaced. "Okay, already. Yes, I was here with Marco on Wednesday. How was I supposed to know he was allergic to shrimp?"

"That's just the thing," I said. "Marco *isn't* allergic. Back in high school, he worked at Frenchy's Shrimp House."

McNulty tilted his head and studied me. "What are you getting at, Fremden?"

"That the dead guy in the box wasn't Marco Shamway." I turned and glared at McLester. "Isn't that right, *Sweet Cheeks*?"

Chapter Forty-Nine

Justice is sweet. But it's even sweeter when the handsome bully who plagued you all through high school now looked like a whimpering manatee. Bonus points to the universe for letting me witness him getting shoved into the back of a police car.

"How did you figure out McLester was actually Shamway?" McNulty asked as we walked over to our vehicles.

"It certainly wasn't his looks," I said. "Actually, it was something he said. Nobody's ever called me Sweet Cheeks except Marco. When he said it this morning, I realized it was him lurking underneath all that blubber."

"Impressive." McNulty pursed his lips. "Your knowledge of Shamway's lack of shrimp allergy seems to substantiate he wasn't the man in the box. But to confirm this guy's Shamway, we need to get him to admit it. Then we need him to tell us who his friend in the box was. Otherwise, we'll have to wait on DNA results."

"Believe me, it's Marco." I nodded at the squad car pulling away with Shamway inside. "What's going to happen to him?"

"That depends. Unless he forced the other man to eat the shrimp salad, there's no murder charges to file. He'll be free to go."

I frowned. "Wait a minute. Are you saying you need another confession from him?"

McNulty eyed me funny. "I suppose, yes."

I smiled coyly. "I think I know how to get it."

• • • •

I WAS AT THE POLICE station talking to Marco Shamway through the bars of a holding cell—only this time, I was on the *outside*.

"We've gotta get you out of here, Marco," I said, pretending to have the hots for him. "But for us to be a real couple, you've gotta come clean with me. Who was the guy in the box?"

Marco let out a huge sigh. "It was Don McLester."

I pretended to swoon and shot Marco my best set of femme fatale doe eyes. "Oh, Marco. You didn't kill him, did you?"

Marco shook his head. "No. I'd never do that, I swear! I didn't know he was allergic to shellfish. Maybe he didn't know either."

"How could that be possible?"

"Don's a greenhorn from North Dakota. He'd never even seen the ocean before."

"And now he never will," I said.

Marco winced. "Honest, Sweet Cheeks, I didn't kill him. All I know is that when we were at that restaurant, Don took a bite of his sandwich and went running off to the restroom. I thought he had diarrhea or something. When he didn't come back, I figured he got lucky with that waitress. Or some chick he met on the way to the toilets. That kind of thing happened to him all the time."

I thought about the image on the billboard. I couldn't blame a gal for taking a shot. "Okay," I said. "But there's something I don't understand. Why did you switch identities with Don?"

"Because when I ran into him one day, he reminded me of how I used to look back in my younger days. For a 40-year-old man, he looked pretty good, don't you think?"

I blanched. "He was *forty*?"

"I know, right? Don was like Tom Cruise. That guy never aged. Not like the rest of us, eh?"

Speak for yourself, jerk!

216

Marco shrugged. "Anyway, when I started this new ad campaign, I hired him to be my public face. As part of the deal, he had to pretend to be me."

I frowned. "And you pretended to be him?"

Marco hung his head like a death row inmate. "Look at me. Do you think anyone would want to buy a Hunk Clock from *me*?"

The man made a serious point.

"Aww, but you're so charming," I lied.

Marco glanced up at me from the bench of his holding cell, tears in his eyes. "You know what? I had a crush on you all through high school."

I nearly swallowed my tonsils. "What?"

He sighed. "But I guess I had a crummy way of showing it."

You aren't kidding.

Marco smiled a faraway smile. "All these years, I never stopped thinking about you. Then, a couple of years ago, I was looking through the yearbook. I saw your school picture and remembered your idea for the Hunk Clock. I thought, this is my big chance to win you over. If I could make a go of it with the *clock*, *you* might have a go at it with *me*."

"Seriously?" I half-whispered, too shocked to know whether to feel flattered or disgusted.

Marco nodded. "Yeah. That's why I put together that contract. To offer you 10% of the royalties."

"Ten percent," I said, and shook my head.

Marco looked down. "I know. It wasn't enough. You deserved it all. That's why I changed the contract to 100%."

My eyebrows shot up. "That wasn't a mistake?"

"No. In fact, I'm giving the *entire business* to you."

I gulped. Maybe Marco Shamway wasn't such a jerk after all.

"Marco, I don't know what to say. Thank you."

He smiled softly, his expression like a lost puppy in the pound. "You're welcome, Sweet Cheeks. You deserve every penny."

Chapter Fifty

"**Y**ou put on quite the show," McNulty said, leading me away from the holding cell area and toward the lobby. "I've got it all on tape. You know, you'd make a pretty decent detective. Or maybe a better con woman."

I grinned. "Really?"

McNulty laughed. "Don't get any ideas, Fremden. Anyway, thanks to the prior background check, we already know who Don McLester is. As soon as we get a DNA match, we can close the case. In the meantime, I'm going to process the paperwork, then set Shamway free."

"Right," I said absently. I chewed my bottom lip.

"What's wrong with you, Fremden? You don't seem very happy for a woman who's just been cleared of murder charges and handed a company worth millions."

"You're right. I don't."

I wonder what's up with that? Geez. I hope it's not my stupid personal integrity raising its ugly head again.

• • • •

ON MY WAY OUT THE DOOR of the police station, I ran into Needra, the wheelbarrow lady.

"Hey!" she said. "I know you. I think I got something you'll like." She reached into her wheelbarrow and pulled out a figurine. "Two bucks and this baby's yours!"

Oddly, even though I was now technically a millionaire, at the moment I didn't have two nickels to rub together. "Sorry, too rich for my blood."

"Aww. You still broke, baby?" she asked. "You can take it on credit!"

"You'd do that?"

"Sure. A bird in the hand, baby. If I don't make a sale, a hundred percent of nothing is still nothing, right? Just write me out an I.O.U."

"Well, okay." I rifled through my purse for a pen and paper. My cell phone rang. It was Finkerman. "Hold on, Needra."

I clicked on the phone. "Finkerman! You won't believe what I'm about to tell you."

"You took the words right out of my mouth," he said. "So, you saw the news?"

I frowned. "What news?"

"It was in this morning's *Jail Bait Journal.* Hunk Clock, Inc. is facing a major lawsuit."

I felt as if I'd been hit in the face with an iron skillet. I could almost hear the *gong* as my fortune went down the drain.

"What?" I squealed. "Why?"

"Shamway's clocks were made in illegal sweatshops," Finkerman said. "And a couple of the components he used are banned by pretty much every country on the planet. We're talking *radioactive*, Fremden."

"Dear lord!" I cried out, causing Needra to gingerly set her figurine back in her wheelbarrow and make a hasty exit down the sidewalk.

"Oh, it gets worse," Finkerman said. "The company owes about four million in back taxes. I hate to say it, but it looks like your 100% of the royalties is gonna be zero."

Needra was right. A hundred percent of nothing is still nothing.

A thought pinged in my brain. My feet broke out in a sweat. "Finkerman? What if the contract had been changed from *royalty shares* to me *owning* the entire company?"

Finkerman laughed. "Good thing that's not the case. Otherwise, you'd be on the hook for it all."

Chapter Fifty-One

I should've known better than to *not* look a gift jackass in the mouth. Just when I'd begun to let my guard down and change my mind about Shamway, he went and scammed me all over again!

Too infuriated to drive, I sat in my car in the police station parking lot, waiting on Finkerman to show up. I hoped against hope that Shamway had been bluffing about having changed the contract to dump the entire Hunk Clock mess in my lap.

• • • •

WHEN FINKERMAN FINALLY arrived at the police station in a rusty orange cloud of smoke, it wasn't good news.

"He really gave you the business, all right," Finkerman said, waving the contract out the window of his Gremlin as I walked up to him. "I don't know how I missed this before."

"Because you were too busy noticing the 100% typo," I said sourly. "Shamway did that intentionally, so you wouldn't bother reading the fine print, and I'd sign it quickly out of greed."

Finkerman whistled and shook his head. "Gotta hand it to him. Greed's an excellent motivator all right. It's the only reason most of us get up in the morning."

I frowned. "What I don't get is why he broke into my house and pretended to care about me."

"The guy's a con man, Fremden. Con stands for *confidence*. It's what these people do. They build your trust so they can lure you in for the swindle."

I gritted my teeth. "Marco needed to dump his dirty business off on a willing sap. *Me*."

"That about sums it up."

"And now I'm totally screwed." I leaned against Finkerman's Gremlin, totally defeated. "You already filed the papers with the courthouse. I'm doomed."

"Not exactly." Finkerman laughed. "I was bluffing you, Fremden. Yesterday was *Saturday*. You think judges work weekends?"

"What?" I squealed and jumped for joy. "Oh, thank you universe!"

"Uh ... not so fast. There's still one fly buzzing around this giant dung heap, so to speak."

"What?" I stopped dancing, reached into the Finkerman's car, and grabbed him by the collar. "What did you do *now*?"

Finkerman grimaced. "I kind of couriered a copy of the contract over to the Don Cesar."

"Oh, crap! To room 22 or 39?"

"McLester's room, 39," Finkerman said. "Why? Are you gonna bust in there and steal it?"

"Don't be ridiculous. I've got an inside man for that." I eyed Finkerman. "Hey, you got fifty bucks on you?"

Chapter Fifty-Two

Finkerman and I returned to the police station in a cloud of smoke, but this time it was *triumphant* smoke.

In a twist of fate, we'd put greed to work for *us*. We'd managed to secure the contract—and my future—by bribing Thonii the hotel concierge. I no longer owed the IRS millions. And it had only cost me a measly Grant.

As it now stood, I only owed Geraldine $45, and Finkerman the $50—plus a debt of gratitude. Despite all odds, the shyster attorney somehow managed to make us both come out smelling like roses.

Now I just had one more greedy man to stick some thorns into the sides of ...

"Thanks, Finkerman," I said, climbing out of his Gremlin. "I owe you one."

"You owe me a lot more than *one*, Fremden. Your tab's up to $407.45."

"How do you figure that?"

"The fifty for Thonii, plus the timing belt."

"Oh, yeah. Fair enough." I leaned my forearm on the ledge of his open driver's window. "Do you take I.O.U.s?"

Finkerman sighed, then reached toward the cracked dash of his Gremlin and grabbed a small receipt pad. "Here. Sign this."

After signing for my debt, I said goodbye to Finkerman and headed into the police station. Tucked under my arm were the only two existing signed copies of the contract that had named me the sole owner of Hunk Clock, Inc.

• • • •

I PAID ONE LAST VISIT to Marco Shamway to deliver the bad news. He didn't take it well.

"No! Stop!" he yelled as I stood in front of his holding cell and tore the contracts to shreds.

"You don't understand," he whimpered, gripping the bars and moaning like a hippo in a Hawaiian shirt. "My whole image will be ruined! My future will be toast!"

"I get it," I said. "I felt the same way all throughout high school, thanks to you." I ripped the last pages of the contracts in half and let them fall into the wastebasket at my feet. "Kiss these babies goodbye, Shamway. They're heading for a nice little bonfire in my backyard tonight."

Shamway shook his head. "You're killing me, Fremden. You're killing me."

I shrugged. "Oh, well. As they say, better you than me, *Sweet Cheeks*."

Chapter Fifty-Three

I turned my back on Shamway and left him wailing inside his holding cell like a wounded wildebeest. Instead of feeling sorry for him, a wellspring of joy pulsed through me. I grinned from ear to ear.

I, Val Fremden, had actually bested Marco Shamway!

I felt like Wonder Woman. My lasso of truth had prevailed! I smiled and thought of Geraldine Jiggles. Just like her, I apparently had my own hidden strength. It might not have been personal integrity, but it sure wasn't nothing.

Could it be gumption?

"Nice work. *Again,*" McNulty said as I passed by his office on the way to the lobby.

I grinned. "If you got that whole thing on tape, I'd love a copy."

He smirked. "I think I can make that happen."

• • • •

AS I WALKED THROUGH the last door separating the inner workings of the police station from the public lobby, I heard a woman yell, "There she is!"

A flash went off in my face.

I blinked against the black dots swirling in my vision. When I could see again, I made out the images of two women gawking at me.

One was a bleach-blonde in her forties. She was holding the kind of big camera members of the media generally carried.

I gasped.

The media? Am I the new town hero?

"That's her! The one they call The Closer," the other woman said, elbowing the camera lady. I recognized her. She was the perky, size-two blonde who'd slammed me at Tiffany's Temps Agency three days ago.

I scowled at the young pipsqueak and her perfect lips and hissed, "What are *you* doing here?"

"*I'm* the new receptionist, Brittany Snows," she said, raising her nose. "What are *you* doing here?"

"I'm Val Fremden," I huffed. "And I just solved a case, if you must know."

"What case?" Brittany asked. She glanced down at the plastic bag full of torn up paper in my hand. "The case of the missing garbage?"

The older woman with the camera snorted with laughter, then froze. "Wait. You're *Val Fremden*? *The* Val Fremden who submitted that idiotic story to the *Beach Gazette* about a pot-bellied pig named Hammy Sandwich?"

The two women looked at each other, then broke out into hysterical laughter.

I felt the heat flare in my cheeks. "How do you know about that?"

The camera lady wiped tears from her eyes. "I'm Shirley Saurwein. Reporter for the *Beach Gazette*. Brittany tipped me off that you were here. I came by to interview you about being the worst temp who ever lived." She turned to Brittany. "What was it Tiffany Darnell called her?"

Brittany smiled cruelly. "The retail version of the Grim Reaper."

"Why you little—" I hissed. But before I could give Miss Goody Two-Size a piece of my mind, a male voice sounded behind me.

"Run that story, Saurwein, and you'll never get another lead from this station again."

I whirled around. McNulty was standing there glaring at Saurwein. I shot him a smile, then turned back just in time to see Saurwein's backside sprinting out the door.

I shot Brittany a *take that you jerk* look, then turned around to thank McNulty. But the cop had slipped away as well. I let out a sigh. It was time to go home.

As I turned toward the door, I thought about my boyfriend, Tom. He'd instructed me not to call him. But since I was already at the police station—and I currently had no active charges or warrants out on me—what was the harm in seeing if he was here? Maybe he could come out and say hi.

"I'd like to speak to Lieutenant Tom Foreman," I told dour-faced Brittany. "Could you buzz him for me, please?"

She sneered. "Do you have an appointment?"

"I don't need an appointment. He's my boyfriend."

She raised a perfect blonde eyebrow, then glanced through the directory. "There's no Tom Foreman listed." She smirked. "Guess that's one deal you *didn't* close, hey?"

"What?" I frowned. "Check again."

She did. Still no Tom.

Blindsided, I stumbled out of the police station into the scorching sun and sweltering heat. What was going on here? Had Tom quit his job and run away with that floozy on the recorder?

He wouldn't do that, would he?

Then it hit me. That little blonde witch of a receptionist was just playing me out of spite.

"Forget her," I muttered. I pulled out my cell phone and marched toward my car. Against Tom's wishes, I called his number. This was an emergency, after all, wasn't it?

I listened as the phone rang once, then clicked over to a recording. "I'm sorry, the number you have dialed has been disconnected or is no longer in service."

No longer in service?

The words rang over and over in my head. I fumbled my way to my car, feeling punched in the gut.

That can't be right.

227

I climbed into Shabby Maggie, my head spinning. As I sat there in shock, I spotted something on the passenger-side floorboard. It was that package I'd tossed into the car on my way back from the mailbox the other day.

I leaned over and grabbed it. Then I turned it over and read the message scrawled on the brown paper wrapping.

Don't open until the big day!

If *today* didn't qualify as the "big day," I didn't know which day ever would.

I tore open the wrapping paper and nearly choked on my own spit. Inside was a Hunk Clock. Stuck to it was a note from Tom.

For when I'm not here to wake you up.

What the heck was *that* supposed to mean?

THE END

Thanks so much for reading *That Time I Kinda Killed a Guy*. It's book one in the *Val Fremden Strikes Again Series*.

If you're new to Val Fremden, you might want to check out her first series, Val Fremden Midlife Mysteries. The nine-book series is available on Amazon. While you're there, I'd be grateful if you took a minute to leave a review for *this* book. I appreciate every single one! Here's a handy link:

https://www.amazon.com/dp/B0C2VZT3LM

Ready for more Val Strikes Again? Awesome! *There's Something About Gary* is the next book in the series. Check out the Sneak Peek included in the back of this book, or read the book description on Amazon by clicking here:

https://www.amazon.com/dp/B0CHWHHTKX

Want to stay in touch and get a laugh in your Facebook feed every day? Join my Facebook page at:

* Facebook: https://www.facebook.com/valandpalspage/

Want to reach me by email or join my newsletter and be the first to hear about new stories coming up? Here you go!

* Newsletter Link: https://dl.bookfunnel.com/fuw7rbfx21
* Website: https://www.margaretlashley.com
* Email: contact@margaretlashley.com

Thanks again. I appreciate you!
All my best,
Margaret

A Sneak Peek at There's Something About Gary

C**hapter One**

The cassette tape in my ancient answering machine *squealed* like an angry chipmunk, perfectly matching my mood. I jabbed the *replay* button for the billionth time and listened yet again to the cryptic message my boyfriend had left me four days ago.

"Val? Hey. It's Tom. I ... um ... kinda got this special assignment. I can't talk about it right now. I'll tell you more later. But I wanted you to know I won't be home tonight. Or maybe for the next few days. Don't call me. I'll call you. Okay. Gotta go."

Then, right at the end, came the infuriating part.

A woman's laugh.

"Tee-hee-hee-hee!"

It was the kind of silly, tinkling laugh only women pretty enough to get by on their looks could pull off. In other words, it sounded nothing like *mine*.

I frowned at the privileged gravitas of the unknown floozy. I pictured her shiny blonde locks. Her ample bosom. Her seductive, pouty lips. My imagination ablaze, I tried to mimic her lilting laugh. What escaped my sour lips sounded more like the bray of an injured donkey.

"A-hee-a-hee-a-hee."

I scowled and mashed the *replay* button again.

In the four-and-a-half years Tom and I'd been together, he'd never pulled anything even remotely like *this* before. At least, not that I'd found out about, anyway. And he certainly had never gone AWOL *for four solid days*.

What in blazes was he up to? Was "special assignment" guy-code for cavorting around with a shameless trollop?

If Tom hadn't been a lieutenant with the St. Petersburg Police Department, I'd have been more worried about his safety. He could've been a victim of foul play, after all.

But after hearing that woman's infuriatingly adorable laugh for the umpteenth time, I figured Tom might actually be better off dead. Because if he was cheating on me, there was a good chance I might murderize the scallywag myself.

• • • •

AFTER 45 YEARS OF FUMBLING my way through a maze of dead-end decisions and wild goose chases, Tom Foreman had been my long-awaited lucky break. Tall, blond, handsome, and good-natured, he'd been a veritable human oasis when I'd washed up back on the shores of my hometown of St. Pete Beach, Florida, five years ago.

Battered and tattered and desperately needing yet another life-saving intervention, I'd run into Tom while committing my first official crime—breaking and entering.

That August morning had been relentlessly hot and humid, just like today. I'd been fumbling around for clues to the rightful heir of Glad Goldrich, an old woman I'd stumbled upon at Sunset Beach.

The first time I'd seen Glad, the scrawny, leather-skinned septuagenarian had been sprawled out on her beach lounger like a dried-up frog. She'd loved the white sand, the warm sun, and an ice-cold Fosters.

And I liked to think she also loved me.

I padded barefoot through my tiny, crackerbox house to my bedroom and plopped onto the edge of the bed. As always, thoughts of Glad brought a wry curl to my lips.

"Screw you, Kiddo," I said, uttering her favorite phrase as I tugged a pair of stretch jeans over my thighs.

As salty as the Gulf of Mexico itself, Glad had wormed her way into my heart, which, believe me, wasn't easy to do. During the six weeks I'd had the privilege to know her, Glad's unfiltered, battering-ram approach to life had turned my victim mentality around. Life was no longer something that happened to me. It was something *I* made happen. Or, at least, I tried to remember that.

When my sassy life coach had died suddenly and left behind unfinished business, I'd felt the need to take charge of the situation. And the way I'd seen it back then, the first order of business was to break into Glad's house.

I shuffled to the bathroom, rubbed on some lip gloss, and sighed at my aging reflection. For decades, I'd tried to master the secrets of the "Makeup Woman" and adopt her mysterious ways. But no matter how I'd tried, I'd never been able to incant the magic spell that turned goop into gorgeous.

With my 50th birthday a fading memory, I'd pretty much given up trying to hide the growing murder of crow's feet tracking steadily across my face. Lip gloss and eyeliner were all I bothered with anymore. Not that it mattered. I mean, as Glad would've said, "Who ya trying to fool, anyway, Kiddo?"

Nobody but myself.

And maybe Tom.

What Tom Foreman saw in me was another mystery I'd yet to crack. I wasn't beautiful, rich, or thin. I chalked up his inexplicable attraction to brain damage caused by some sort of head injury. But whatever odd magnetism I held over the man, he'd been possessed by it from the moment we'd met.

I knew this because that day I'd broken into Glad's house, Tom hadn't arrested me. Instead, like a rogue prince from a fractured fairytale, the cop had actually stood guard while I and a couple of pals had rummaged through Glad's place!

Anyway, that's how Tom and I'd officially met. How we were officially going to part, however, was now as dangerously up in the air as a clay pigeon at a skeet shoot.

So much for happily ever after.

I stopped scowling at myself in the bathroom mirror and flipped off the light. Figuring out what I was going to do about Tom would have to wait—I had an even more pressing crisis to deal with. If I didn't hustle, I was going to be late for work. And given my appalling employment history, that was a mistake I absolutely could *not* afford to make.

I inched my way into a pair of cheap rubber sandals, grabbed the keys to Shabby Maggie (my rusty old Ford Falcon convertible) and headed for the door.

My current job might not have been glamorous, but it kept Maggie's tank half full. And, more importantly, it kept me out of jail for shoplifting—a charge as trumped up as the wad of skunk hair adorning my new boss's withered old head.

Ancient, crafty, and shady as all get-out, Geraldine Jiggles had accused me of stealing a Hummel figurine from her thrift store. Then she'd threatened to call the cops on me if I didn't cover her shifts so she could attend a slots tournament in Vegas.

In other words, the old bat had blackmailed me into working for her at Belated Rooms, the junk shop she owned on Corey Avenue.

How the scummy old store's name had come to include the word "belated," I had no idea. All I knew for sure was that if I showed up late for work again, my forthcoming obituary would surely include the word "beheaded."

Keep the laughs rolling. Check out **There's Something About Gary** on Amazon now!

https://www.amazon.com/dp/B0CHWHHTKX

About the Author

W hy do I love underdogs?

Well, it takes one to know one. Like the main characters in my novels, I haven't led a life of wealth or luxury. In fact, as it stands now, I'm set to inherit a half-eaten jar of Cheez Whiz...if my siblings don't beat me to it.

During my illustrious career, I've been a roller-skating waitress, an actuarial assistant, an advertising copywriter, a real estate agent, a house flipper, an organic farmer, and a traveling vagabond/truth seeker. But no matter where I've gone or what I've done, I've always felt like a weirdo.

I've learned a heck of a lot in my life. But getting to know myself has been my greatest journey. Today, I know I'm smart. I'm direct. I'm jaded. I'm hopeful. I'm funny. I'm fierce. I'm a pushover. And I have a laugh that lures strangers over, wanting to join in the fun.

In other words, I'm a jumble of opposing talents and flaws and emotions. And it's all good.

I enjoy underdogs because we've got spunk. And hope. And secrets that drive us to be different from the rest.

So dare to be different. It's the only way to be!

All my best,

Margaret

Made in the USA
Las Vegas, NV
08 October 2024

96509051R00139